Pride Publishing books by BA Tortuga

Single Books
What She Wants

Roughstock
Blind Ride
And a Smile
File Gumbo
Coke's Clown
Back to Back
Pulled from All Sides
Leading the Blind

Rocking W
The Wounded Warrior

Roughstock

LEADING THE BLIND

BA TORTUGA

Leading the Blind
ISBN # 978-1-83943-989-6

Interior text design by Claire Siemaszkiewicz
Pride Publishing

Published in 2021 by Pride Publishing, United Kingdom.

Pride Publishing is an imprint of Totally Entwined Group Limited.

LEADING THE BLIND

Dedication

To my fans. You kept the flame lit. I couldn't do this without all y'all. Much love, BA
Special thanks to Jaymi and Rachel for their help.

Chapter One

"Jesus fucking Christ! Open your goddamn eyes next time! That bull damn near rang your bell." Bax shook his arm, and Jason swore that made the world swim before his useless fucking eyes again.

"Andy Baxter, you'd best back the fuck off. This ain't the time." He'd know Coke's voice anywhere, the bullfighter as much a part of his family as anyone ever had been.

"Gramps, don't." Jason Scott leaned against the stall, breathing hard. The last thing he needed was Pa and Ma MacGillicuddy freaking out because he'd lost his cookies at a bull riding. Bull riding fans were a specific breed, and it didn't matter one bit whether it was the big show or a tiny two-gate sheriff's posse arena. They all talked.

"Well, someone has to," Coke ground out. "He's being an ass."

"He needs to keep his eyes open." But Bax lowered his voice, thank God.

"I know. I got dirt in 'em. It's not like I can wipe them, Bax."

"For eight seconds, you can suck it up."

"Right. 'Cause you were always fucking perfect."

Bax grabbed his shirtfront and shook him. "Every. Fucking. Ride."

"Stop it," Coke snapped, and they stopped. Gramps rarely spoke in that tone. When he did, well, they listened. "Y'all are being buttheads and I don't need this shit, you *comprende*? Folks got phones."

"Sorry," Bax murmured, which made Jason snort.

"Don't tease the bull, son. Tell Andy you're sorry."

Jason blew out a hard breath. "You know I am, butthead."

"Good boys. Come on now. We got to get out of the public." Coke tugged at his arm. Hell, Coke had to get back to work.

"Right. I'm going to get out of here, Gramps. I sure as shit ain't making the short go."

"Okay, son." Coke clapped him on the back. "Be good."

Bax laughed. "Right. He'll be trying to drive off in the truck soon."

"I'd do better than some." His head was starting to pound like there was a damn mariachi band in there, playing away.

"You did okay last time," Bax agreed, taking his arm and leading him out of the arena. "Until you didn't."

"Story of my life." He rode like a champion, until he didn't. He could see, until he couldn't. He had a whole life, until it was over. Now? He was fixin' to try and take some of it back.

"Hey, I just want you to be safe."

"I know. I just want you to not have to babysit my ass forever."

"I'm not your babysitter." Bax lowered his voice. "I'm yours, and we're in this together, Mini."

Jason felt his fucking shoulders come down from around his ears. *Okay. Yeah.* 'Together' he could get behind. *A burden?* No, that he couldn't do. "Right. Sorry. You want a beer?" *An aspirin? Something to stop this pounding?*

"Sure. Sounds good." Bax led him out of the arena, the dirt changing to concrete.

He tried to make sure his face was thunderous, keeping anyone away who might want to talk. He was getting better at that part—the talking to fans—but not much. Right now he thought he might die if someone stopped them. Bax kept him moving fast, and soon enough he was in the cab of their truck, the sudden quiet shocking his senses.

"I'm taking you to the travel trailer, okay?" Bax sounded either pissed or scared. He wasn't sure which.

"Okay." Jason didn't want to fight no more, so he folded his hands and sat quiet as a mouse.

They didn't play music, they just drove, and when they got to the gravel road, Jason knew they were at the weird little campground.

The truck rocked a bit when Bax hit the brakes. The engine cut off, and they sat there.

"You okay?" Bax finally asked.

"My head hurts some," he admitted. "I need some time to not worry about shit."

"Well, come on. We'll get you some pills and watch a movie."

Listen to a movie, more like, but whatever. "Works for me."

"You sure? I could put on one of those audiobooks."

"I just want to be somewhere I" —*can see*— "know."

"It's cool and quiet in there." Bax climbed out of the truck, then came around to help him out.

"Yeah." He sighed. "I'm sorry, Bax."

"What for, Mini?" They stepped up into the trailer, the smell oddly homey inside.

"Being blind?" *Having you take care of me when all I want in all the world is to take care of you.*

"Well, that's stupid. Ain't like you asked to be blind."

"No." *No, not a bit.* "Good thing we cleared that up."

"You know it." Bax snorted loud, then guided him to sit back on the bed thingy. "Let me get us a cold drink, then we can kinda float."

"Thanks. I'll get the next one." He toed his boots off and stripped out of his sponsor shirt and his baggy, filthy work jeans.

"No problem." Bax opened a couple of bottles, the bottle cap sound unmistakable.

He took the bottle when Bax offered it and drank deep, the lemon-lime bubbles suiting him to the bone.

"Mmm. It was dry as dirt out there, huh?"

"Yeah. Yeah, and I'm pretty sure my mouth was open when I hit the ground." His molars were a little gritty.

"Ew. No cow shit, Mini."

Jason snorted, tickled shitless. "No. Although God knows how much we've eaten accidentally over the years."

"Stop." Bax pinched his hip. "That's nasty."

"No pinching!" He rolled toward Bax, trying not to spill his drink. "You're such a wuss."

"I am not. I swim with you at your momma's place. There's snake poop in there." Bax had a point there. Jason wasn't real sure what the point was, but Bax had one.

"I don't even want to think about what all is in that pond, Bax."

"Nope."

They kinda…lounged. Just sat there and breathed like great big lazy gators. He laughed a little at that. Gators did okay blind, according to Beau Lafitte.

"What's funny, Mini?"

"Alligators."

"That ain't funny. That's a lot of teeth."

"You're just grumpy. Most days they're funny."

"Kinda, yeah." Bax took his hand. "Sorry I yelled, Mini."

"I'm trying. I swear to God. I'm trying hard to do this." And God knew there were more than a few days when he just wanted to give up, to go home to Momma's and admit defeat. Shit fire and save matches, what the fuck was he thinking, riding blind? He'd got his bell rung when he could see.

"I know. I know it." Bax sighed. "I want— Shit, Mini, I want you to be happy, and you're not."

"I don't want to ride the little events forever. I don't want to be a has-been." He didn't want to be a burden.

"You're not. You're doing amazing."

Now, Bax wasn't one to blow smoke up anyone's ass, so the words perked him up a little bit.

"You think so? I feel like a fuck-up."

"That's because we're all always telling you what to do."

He traced Bax's fingers, one after another. Lord have mercy, those calluses felt like heaven when they touched him. The fact that they'd never touched him when he couldn't see wasn't lost on him. Bax had saved him. Completely. Fucker.

"You're pouring smoke, Jason. Out of your brain." Bax chuckled. "Thinkin' ain't what we do best."

"Fuck no. We do stupid shit and drink beer." It was the cowboy way, after all.

"See? I knew it." Bax rolled to kiss his cheek.

"Knew what?" He could meet Bax halfway.

"That we're better not thinking." Bax laughed, poking his ribs.

He chuckled. "No shit on that, man."

"Mmm." Bax settled in right against his hip. "I got you, Jason. You just scared me, is all."

"Scared me too. I hate being this way."

"I know." Those fingers moved over him, Bax stroking his belly.

Goosepimples climbed up his skin, heading from hips to nipples. "Mmm. I don't hate this, though."

"No, sir. I love this. Holding you. Touching you."

"Good deal."

Bax was breathing, steady and sure, and the rhythm liked to hypnotized him. "That is a good deal," Bax agreed.

"We are. I mean, this is. Us. Christ."

"It is what it is." That was right down Zen of Bax.

He nodded and let his eyes close. It was the only way he could see colors. Sometimes he thought he could see Bax. Sometimes he knew he could.

"You're smiling." Bax rewarded him with a kiss.

He didn't say why, and it didn't matter. Nothing he did would change his world. No sense getting Bax's hopes up.

Together, they'd get through today. Tomorrow too.

The day after that would just have to take care of itself.

Chapter Two

Bax loved the travel trailer. It took all the hotel pressure off them. No one would bother them at the campground, and the guys all hated the tiny space. Mini felt more comfortable too, and that relaxation suited Bax to the bone.

"You ready to stop for the night, Mini?" Bax glanced over at the passenger seat of the truck.

"I am, yeah. Where are we?"

"Uh. Somewhere outside of Tulsa."

"Cool. Flat and green." Mini's eyes were open, following the shadows.

Bax turned back to the road. Trying to see if Jason actually noticed anything could make a man nuts. "Yeah. Weather's pretty nice, too. We should grab a burger before we stop and have a little picnic."

"Sounds good to me. I love springtime."

Yeah. Bax smiled, happy he'd hit on the right thing. Mini could swing from one mood to another in seconds these days. It was a little like a video game.

Part of him—a real secret, damn near silent because Mini would kill him part—wondered if it wouldn't have been good to get Jason some help, a head-shrinker, something. Wasn't no way Jason Scott would see one of them doctors, but Bax could wish. And if wishes were horses, then beggars would ride.

"You're awful quiet. You cool?" Oh, that one leg was starting to bounce. Someone was getting bored.

Good time to stop.

"I'm fine. Got to pee." That was the truth.

"Me too." Mini worked that little bent nail puzzle around and around, solving it, resetting it, solving it. *Time to find another one.* Anything Jason could do by touch worked, and those puzzles were a staple of Cracker Barrels all over. Bax liked to hold hands with Jason when they walked in the door. The looks were worth a fucking fortune.

He chuckled, which made Jason smile.

"So, we got Burger King, Jack in the Box and Popeyes."

"Burger King... Oh, but Popeyes has the onion rings..."

"And the red beans and rice." Mini would eat with a fork just fine when it was only them.

Jason nodded to him. "And the biscuits. We could get enough for breakfast."

"We so could." Some extra chicken fingers and packets of honey and they'd be better than Whataburger. "We'll do that. Save our cereal for another day."

"Cool." Now Jason was simply beaming, his face turned up to the sun that was coming through the windows.

Score one for Bax. It made him stupidly happy, that grin. He reached over, put a hand on Mini's leg, and Jason dropped one hand over his.

"Feels good."

"Yeah?" They coasted to a stop at Popeyes. "You want to sit?"

"We're going to take it for a picnic, right?"

"Yeah."

"Then I better sit."

Christ, Mini had to have a bladder that could hold a gallon. He'd go at the KOA, Bax reckoned.

"Okay. Back in a flash." He squeezed Jason's leg.

He hit the head then ordered a bunch—chicken fingers and onion rings and rice and beans and a dozen of those biscuits. Bax got two iced teas and a Dr Pepper, then stopped to get mustard and honey. They must think he was feeding an army, not the tiniest bull rider alive. Bax shook his head. Mini had lost weight since they'd started training again. Man never bulked up like he did. It wouldn't matter, except the son of a bitch ate like a horse. Bax tried not to have a jealous bone, but God knew he was gonna end up one of them cowboys who had to buy new Wranglers once a year because he outgrew 'em. Mini was gonna have to work on not fading away.

He grabbed all the bags so he could head back to the truck.

Mini was waiting, and some old cowboy was at the window, jabbering away. Mini was still, stiff around the fake smile.

"Hey, there. Anything I can do for you?" Bax asked, trying not to look like he was running.

"I was just talking to Mr. Scott here. I couldn't believe it was him, but it was."

"Yep. In the flesh. Andy Baxter, sir. Pleased to meet you." He pushed the bags into the truck cab and Mini took them. "Take the drinks too, huh?"

"Sure. Sure, man." There was a metric fuck-ton of stress in Jason's voice.

"Well, it's nice to meet you too, Mr. Baxter. I saw you ride Buzzsaw in Oklahoma City."

Bax let out a real laugh. "That was a heck of a ride."

"Yessir. I thought you had your chickens scrambled for sure."

"Well, we sure appreciate you watching the shows, sir." Bax hoped the feller got the message.

"Are y'all heading to the bull riding in Tulsa?"

"We are. Just a small event, but you know Jason was hurt pretty bad." He hated saying it, but a reminder to fans would give them time.

"I know. I was there. Worried us all bad. We're glad to see you coming back."

"Thank you, sir." Jason clutched the bags of food like a drowning man.

"Well, I'll let you boys eat." The old guy slapped the side of the truck.

"Have a good one," Bax said before climbing into the cab. "You need to roll up the window, Mi-Jase."

"My hands are full. Can you just drive, please?"

"Sure." He got the wheels moving. "You did great."

"Yeah?"

Mini relaxed at his words.

"He had no clue." Bax chuckled. "Good thing I got there before he asked you to sign anything."

"No shit on that. I thought it was you knocking." Jason swallowed hard, shook his head. "I just… Damn."

"It's bound to happen." A lot…and Bax knew it. "Better one feller than twenty."

"Yeah. I got this."

Which was a lie and they both knew it, but what was he going to say? He just grunted. Then he found a place to pull off so they could eat. It would be cold before they got to the campground.

He took the bags from Jason and started getting stuff out. "You want ranch for the onion rings?"

"Nah. Plain is fine."

"Okay. But I got some, and I'll have it open if you want any." He had one of those glove box trays that had a drink holder and all, that Jase could fold down. AJ's buddy from high school, Carter Mason, did car detailing, so it had been easy-peasy.

Jason found the food with his fingers and ate a couple of onion rings without a fucking word.

He tried not to sigh. Jason had been so excited about Popeyes. Now he was wigged out.

God, what the fuck were they doing? What the fuck was he thinking, letting Pharris convince Jason that he could do this?

"I'm okay, Bax." Jason reached over and touched his wrist, his fingers a little greasy. Offering him comfort, and didn't that make him feel guilty as hell? "Just wore out. It ain't no thing."

"We're about to go rest." He opened the box of chicken. "Here, Mini. Have a bite." Bax would get out a biscuit next.

"Is it going to be like this forever, you think?"

"Shut up and eat, Mini." He didn't have no more answers than anybody. He didn't know. Maybe he needed to ask around, see what kind of training Jason was supposed to be having. Shit, who was he kidding? He'd have to google it.

Dear Google, How the fuck do I help a guy who's trying to pretend he ain't blind?

Right.

Fuck.

He nibbled a chicken finger. Might as well get them to the campground. "We'll heat all this up, huh?"

"Yeah." Jason carefully refolded the box of onion rings.

"You can have all you want. I was just kind of thinking we'd eat while it was hot, but we should get comfy." Bax always felt like he had to overexplain, since Jase couldn't see his face.

"You didn't sign on for this, Bax. I know you didn't."

Bax got the wheels rolling again. "I was always yours."

"Always is a long time."

"Yep. Even when I didn't admit it, I was yours." Bax shrugged. "It's just that simple."

"Okay." And there it was.

Whatever they had to figure, from fans to chicken fingers, Andy Baxter was all in.

They'd figure it out or they would go down in flames.

One way or the other, they'd be fine.

* * * *

Once they stopped and he got in the trailer, Jason thought he could breathe. This was familiar, easy. He felt like he knew where he was, where everything was. Like he could eat.

Bax heated up the food in the little toaster oven, which got the crispy stuff crispy again. *Yum.* The biscuits and red beans went into the microwave.

"Smells good. Smells *real* good." He pulled out paper plates and forks, then found the ranch in the mini fridge.

"It does, huh?" Bax sounded pretty happy, which was good.

He put the plates and stuff on the table, then went to the microwave and waited for the beep.

"You want some ranch now? I got butter out for the biscuits."

"I want both. I got the ranch already."

"Well, look at you," Bax teased. "All efficient."

"Shut up, you butthead."

He laughed though, didn't he?

"Mmm. Make me." Bax swung him around, the tiny space in the trailer leaving him nowhere to go. He let it happen, knowing that Bax had him. All he had to do was keep his eyes open.

Bax kissed him, really letting him feel it. *Oh. Oh, hello.* He blinked, trying to catch a glimpse, something.

"Hey, just relax, Mini."

"I am. I want to see you kiss me."

"I want that, too. So bad." Bax rested their foreheads together.

"I want another kiss worse."

"That I can do." Bax kissed him until his ears rang, and he held on, begging for one more, another. More. The damn food could wait again. "You hungry, Mini?"

"Uh-huh." He was starving for Bax's touch. He reached up to hold them together, to make sure Bax knew. "I got you."

Jason pressed one leg between Bax's thighs, rocking them together.

"Hell yes." Bax was panting already, so hot off the mark, and Jason leaned in to take another of those wild kisses. Bax rubbed on him, hard as hell through those starched jeans, so he worked one hand between them, squeezing hard. "Oh." Bax made a noise, hot as hell and twice as deep. He wanted to hear that again. Needed to. He needed to know he could make Bax wild.

If he couldn't do anything else in this life, he could love this man to death.

"More, Mini. Please." Bax sounded hoarse and needy. *Perfect.*

"All of it," he promised, and he yanked at Bax's buckle, his fingers tracing it. West Texas. He knew this one.

"That's it." Bax sucked in so he could undo the button and zipper.

"You smell good," he whispered, so low. It was true—it was Ivory soap and leather and musk and it made his mouth dry.

"Yeah, well, you taste good."

He snorted, the sound strangled as he grabbed Bax's cock.

"Mmm." Bax rose up against him, probably going on his tiptoes.

"Pretty, pretty." Bax was solid in his palm, hot as a brand.

"Want you. I—damn, Mini. Need."

"Good." He stroked, up and down, making Bax feel every callus.

"So good. So." Bax tugged at his shirt.

"So." If he stripped off, he'd have to lose his prize.

"Mini. I want to touch."

"Uh-huh. I want everything." He let go and yanked his shirt off. Then he reached unerringly for that hard flesh he needed.

Bax touched him, sliding those callused hands on his arms, his shoulders, and he moaned his pleasure. "Mmm. Hello."

He did like Andy Baxter's hands, no question.

"I swear, you need sun, Mini. You're gonna glow like Gramps' ass."

Butthead man. He didn't have a lot of time nekkid outside. "We ought to go to Gramps'. Use the pool."

"Not now." Bax laughed, pinching one of Jason's nipples.

"No. No, not now. No pinching, you turd." He dragged his thumb over Bax's slit hard enough that the bastard would feel it.

"No?" It became a two-syllable word, the end note rising right up.

Oh now, that was so fun that he did it again.

"Mini!" Bax leaned close, nipping at his lower lip.

His breath hitched in his chest at the sting. "Yeah, Bax?"

"Hot. God, you make me crazy." Bax went for his buckle like there wasn't nothing else the man wanted on earth.

Good. Good. He needed that. Needed to be the one who was turning Bax's knobs. The only one, though he never doubted that. Andy Baxter would kick the ass of any other man who tried to touch him…assuming Jason didn't get to them first.

He chuckled, stroking up and down, working his thumb over the head of Bax's cock. Bax began to squeeze, digging his fingers in and relaxing, over and over. Jason thought he could hear Bax's heartbeat, thundering along. He closed his eyes, focusing on touch and smell, on the way Bax moaned. He reached around with his free hand so he could grab that tight, hard ass. Bax might not be riding now, but he worked out daily with Jason, and it showed. The extra weight, the extra muscle—it suited Bax down to the bone.

He squeezed both his handfuls, humming at the way Bax danced for him.

"Don't you stop, man. I need this."

Jason didn't have any intention of stopping. No, sir, he was going to see this to the very end. "Got no reason to stop."

"And a million to keep going." Bax shoved down Jason's jeans, so now both of them would fall right over if they tried to move.

"Uh-huh." Eyes open. Balance. Stroke. Focus.

"Shhh. I got you, Mini. I ain't gonna let you fall."

He fucking loved that, how Bax knew. They were damn in tune these days. Bax slid one arm around him, solid as a rock.

"Not even when I make you shoot?"

Bax grunted, pushing into his hand. "Nope. I'm like a mountain."

"Mmhmm. A mountain with peaks." He stroked like he knew Bax needed it, base to tip.

That made Bax chuckle, humping hard, begging with that whole body. He swore he could smell how much Bax needed. He felt it, too, the tiny drops Bax released coating his fingers.

He lifted his fingers to his mouth, licking them clean, before going back to work.

"Oh, fuck." Bax squeezed him so tight that he lost the ability to breathe a moment.

"Kiss me. Kiss me, Bax."

Bax kissed him, giving him everything he needed. Those lips felt so hot yet soft, and Bax pushed in with his tongue, fucking Jason's mouth. He matched the rhythm, jacking Bax steadily.

"Mmm." Bax kept one arm around him but reached down to grasp his cock with the other, so he gasped, fighting to keep his balance. Bax held him strong, keeping him from tipping. "I said I got you."

"I know. Thank God." If they fell, they'd rip each other's dicks off.

Bax huffed out a laugh, rubbing him harder, then shifting suddenly so their cocks were together.

"Oh." That pressure was better, the feel of Bax's shaft alongside his stealing his breath.

"Uhn. Uh-huh."

Together they made everything feel bigger, wilder. Better. He knew both of them were going to come soon, and Jason held on, clinging to Bax. He closed his eyes because he had to.

"I have you. Come on. Come on, Mini."

"Bax!" He let go, shooting hard, letting Bax keep him upright.

"Yes." The sharp word was bitten out. Bax was right there, and as soon as he finished, Jason felt Bax's wet heat spill onto his arm.

He swayed, sucking in sex-filled air. *Damn, that felt good.*

"Uhn." Bax licked his lips, loving on him slow and steady.

Lord, he was dizzy as all get out and it felt so good. "Uh-huh."

"God, yes. Okay, Mini. Open your eyes and hold my shoulders, huh?" Bax eased down to push off his boots and jeans.

He wasn't having kinky thoughts about Bax on his knees. He wasn't. "Mmm."

"Hush, you." Bax laughed, breath hot on his thighs.

"Hmm?" He went for innocent, because that was all he had.

"Right." Bax got all the extra clothes off them, then stood again. "Safe now."

He went for a bull-rider pose, all spread and cocked hips. "Am I?"

"You are. Amazing, too." Bax petted his belly.

Jason flushed, then pulled Bax up. "Let's eat and build our energy up for round two."

See him, see him be daring as all fuck.

"I like it." Bax laughed right out loud, the sound relaxed and happy.

"Aren't we happy as a dog with two tails?"

"Yep. I feel amazing." Bax took his hand, leading him to go sit on the bed. "I'll grab the feast."

"Perfect." He pushed the sheets around, making what felt like a decent place to serve the food. Flat, at least. Both he and Bax sucked at making the bed. After all, folks just unmade it every damn day, didn't they? *Yes. Yes, they did.* Seemed like a big old waste of time, even when a feller could see it.

"I cain't believe we're fixin' to eat sitting here all nekkid." Bax sounded tickled as all get out.

"I won't tell." He wanted to see it so bad.

"No. I'm not sharing this. This is all mine."

He reached out, and Bax took his hand.

"I mean it, Mini. I wanted this so long and I finally got my shits together. I'm never letting go."

He grinned, and it spread on his face until his cheeks hurt. "Promise."

"I swear to God."

That was enough for him, wasn't it? *Yessir.*

The food suddenly smelled and tasted way better than it had in the truck.

He could live with that.

Chapter Three

Bax used to love staying at hotels while they were on tour. Once upon a time he'd never have missed an after-party or a buffet. Now hotels were kind of a logistical clusterfuck. Jason had to get in and out without other cowboys or fans bothering him. There was no sitting at the bar, going to the restaurant—and the after-parties? *Jesus Christ, what a* nightmare.

"You ready to go in?" Jason asked.

"I am." He just needed to put on his happy face.

"Good deal. Let's do this." Okay, Jase was in fierce mode.

That was usually good *and* bad. They hopped out of the truck, which was where AJ Gardner met them. "Howdy, boys."

"Hey, Aje. What's the lay of the land?" Jason held one hand out to shake.

"Pretty busy in there. Mostly older fans instead of buckle bunnies, so be careful."

"Right. Registration straight ahead?"

"Yep. I'll buy you a beer later, huh?"

"Yeah. Yeah, sounds great." Jason smiled, grabbed his duffel and pulled his hat down. "Let's do this."

"Works for me." Bax would tell Jason who to acknowledge. "I'll do the check-in. You want to sit in the lobby?"

"That's prob'ly my safest bet, huh?"

"Yeah." Bax led Jason to a chair, letting him ease down before dropping the bags at his feet. "Be right back."

"I got this."

Bax sure as shit hoped so, because there were two old men heading over to talk to Jase. He had to let Jason do this, though. Had to. If Jason couldn't fool some fans, he would never work the big show.

He checked in, forcing himself not to look back over and over. No, Mini had to get this down. This was the easy part. Jason knew how to bullshit, knew how to listen. He could do this.

When Bax finally got their room key, he turned around to find Brian Taggart standing there with the two old guys, laughing, and Jason was smiling.

Relief flooded him, and he found himself grinning.

He wandered over. "Bri, good to see you." He shook hands, then offered a hand to the nearest older gent. "Andy Baxter."

"Oh, damn. The whole world is here. I'm Parker Malloy. I'm pleased to meet y'all."

"Same to you, sir."

The other feller stuck out his big paw. "Tom O'Dell."

"Mr. O'Dell." He shook. "Are y'all here for the bull riding?"

"We are. Figured we might as well."

Bax loved how casual that sounded.

"I think it'll be a good event." Jase nodded, keeping his dark glasses on.

Brian chuckled. "You got the best safety man in the business, at least."

Jason grinned slow. "Oh, is Adam here?"

"Little fucker." Brian flipped Jason off. "He's working the big show."

"Mmm, where the real bull riders go." Bax laughed at the expressions on the fans' faces. "We tease because we care."

"Are y'all riding to get back up there?" O'Dell asked, and Andy was shocked as hell to see Jason nod.

"I just have a few events and I'm in the money."

He sucked in a deep breath, hoping it didn't show. He thought they were doing a whole season down here…

Wasn't that the plan? Had Jase been planning shit without him?

He bit his tongue. Bax would jump Jason in the elevator.

"Good deal. You're a natural. I always put money on you when you ride." The old man was sharp, eyes watching everything.

"Thank you, sir. You ready to take the bags up, Bax? AJ wants to buy us that beer."

"Nice meeting you," Bax told the others. "Brian, see you in a bit."

"I'll holler and come up."

Jason stood, nodded, and grabbed the bags.

Bax moved in, he hoped unobtrusively, to help guide Jason on the way to the elevators.

"Did I do okay?" Jase whispered.

"You did." That was the truth. Jason had rocked it.

Jason beamed at him, and the elevator dinged open. Jason waited until the doors opened, tilting his head as he listened. Bax let Jason go through, thankful no one else was with them, and Jason seemed confident as hell, heading into the elevator.

The door slid closed, though, and Jason sighed. "That was good, right?"

"Uh-huh. You really planning to level up?"

"I think I'm going to have to try soon. I can't keep fooling folks for years. I'm not there yet, though."

"No." That was true enough, he supposed. He needed to talk to Coke.

"We need to be able to get help, Bax. You know? We have to, so that I can be with you, where I'm worth something."

What? "You're everything to me." He guessed he got it, though. A man had his pride.

"I know, but you didn't take me to raise. I want you to be able to…have fun. I want us to be able to relax together."

"Okay. I can get that, Mini. Not to mention, you win a few and Ace Porter will call."

Jason rolled his eyes, which Bax had to admit he'd guessed by the eyebrows, because he couldn't tell in the dark glasses. "Yeah. Gramps says it's already come up a couple of times."

"Shit." Okay, so they had to step up the plan. They could do this.

The elevator beeped and they headed out. There were people in the hall, talking loudly, and Jason's steps faltered.

"Excuse us." Bax let Jason focus on his voice, which made it easier to track, and thank God, Jason nodded and followed. "We're in six-o-four, man. I hope that's near the ice machine."

"Me, too. I hate to trek for an hour."

"Jason! Hey." The voice was familiar, but Bax had to turn to look to see who. Bonner. The kid had helped Coke out a lot back when he'd broke his neck. *Right.*

Jason tilted his head. "Hey, Bonner?"

"Yeah. How goes it? I haven't seen your ass in a month of Sundays."

"I been working my way back up."

"Good deal. We've missed you. You, too, Andy."

Bax made a wry face. "Gee, thanks."

Jason chuckled softly and shook his head. "Bax is still recovering."

Right. Recovering. Try retired. His leg was held together with baling wire and duct tape. Lord knew it wouldn't even hold his weight some days, especially when the weather was bad. Not only that, but Mini was his full-time job.

They said it was good when someone loved what they did.

"There's a bunch of us going for a beer tonight, if y'all want to come," Bonner offered.

"Been a long day of driving. We'll see, huh?" Bax would let Jason decide, but Jason had a rep for staying in anyway. There was no way Mini would be out at a loud bar. No way.

"Yeah, give us a holler."

Andy could see Mini's tension in the way he held his lips.

"We'll see," Jason murmured. "Later, man."

"Later!" Bonner bounced off, and Jason drew in a deep breath.

"Two more doors." Bax took Jason's elbow to guide him to their room.

"Two more doors." As soon as Jason got in, he relaxed, damn near melted.

"See? You did grand." Bax hugged Jason tight.

"Thanks. I managed okay, huh?"

"You did. If they don't got room service, I vote for pizza."

"Pizza works for me." Jason leaned into him. "Christ on a pink sparkly crutch, it's hot in here."

"Let me get the air going," Bax said, hunting for the wall unit. The damn thing was turned off, and he turned it to high.

"Oh, I can feel that already." Mini grinned and lifted his face toward the air.

"I know, right? Man, they just make these rooms so hot." He watched Jason strip off his shirt, giving him the view of that perfectly flat belly, the trail to glory that was for him and him alone.

Bax stifled a moan. Mini needed to rest up for the event, not have hot monkey sex. *Right?*

Jason tilted his head, listening to him. Hearing him.

Bax grinned. "So not fair, you hearing so much better now."

"Mmm. I like your sounds. Knowing what they mean and shit."

He drifted over to Mini, his hands itching to touch. "Yeah?"

"Uh-huh." Jason's eyes closed and he breathed in deep, a smile starting to cross his face. "I can smell you, too."

"Can you? Do I smell gross?" Travel could do that.

"No sir. You smell like mine…and horny."

"Oh." Bax chuckled, then swooped right in for a kiss. It still made his balls draw up, every single time. This was real and he needed it bad. He hated that Jason was blind, but he was grateful for this love every day. Every single one. Jason stepped into him and groaned, one leg pressing in between his thighs.

"Hey, you." He said it against Jason's mouth.

"Hey, Bax. I want you."

Oh, didn't he love those words in Jason's voice?

"Good deal. I want you, too." He took another kiss, then another, shutting out everything else.

Jason stripped him down like nothing going, the fine son of a bitch not the least bit clumsy, those fingers knowing just what they were doing. This, they had practice at. Lots of it.

He watched Jase like a hawk—the expressions that crossed Jason's lean face fascinated the living fuck out of him. It was like before everything had been a lie, everything had been hidden away—and now he could see anything he wanted. It wasn't true. He'd seen Jase staring at him, lusting after him before, but he hadn't been brave enough to reach. Not before he'd known that Jase might well and truly leave his happy ass.

Now he held on with both hands. This time he kissed hard and told Mini how he felt.

He could feel that hard heat, the pressure against his thigh that proved Jason's need. Bax rocked against Jason, his moan coming right out loud now. That felt so fine.

"Mmm. Mine."

"Well, duh." Who else's would he possibly be?

"Not romantic." Jason pinched his hip.

"Because romance, that's me." He spun Jason around, his cock grinding into that sweet bubble butt.

"Dancing with me."

"Uh-huh. You know how I like to dance." Bax could cut a rug.

"I do."

He slid one hand down, letting his thumb catch on Jase's hipbone and the rest of his hand just frame all that goodness behind Mini's zipper.

"Uhn." Jason rolled his hips, grinding a little.

Dancing. That was what they needed. A dance. A fuck. A nap. In that order. Bax swayed, then turned Jason, leading him around the room a little. Music? They didn't need no stinking music.

Of course, he'd take it when Jason started humming an old George tune. Damn, that sounded sweet as fuck. He did love those moments when Mini sang. Maybe that would be Jason's second career, huh? His Mini, country music sensation.

Bah. He wanted a ranch with some waterfront and a shit ton of cattle and dogs.

Bax turned Jason to face him and broke into a two-step. Jason smiled and let him lead, the motion easy as breathing, which was a dumb goddamn thing to think, because suddenly he couldn't. Suddenly he was fighting to suck in air because they were dancing.

"You okay?" Jason reached up to stroke his cheek, his hand steady as could be.

"I am." He wasn't, but that wasn't Mini's fault.

"Cool. I like this."

"Me, too." God, did he. He loved the feel of Jason sliding against him, loved the smile Mini wore. Loved how Jason believed in him, without question.

They wound down to a waltz, and the urgency had slid past now. Oh, they'd love on each other, but it could wait.

"You really thinking to move up, Mini? For real?"

"I only got so much time, Bax. I cain't hide this forever."

"I know. I just hate it's not fair to you. You should be able to let people know. Other than that, I'm behind you one hundred percent." *Always.*

"Momma would say life's not fair."

"She's right. It sucks. But I got you here. Now."

"You do. Praise God and Greyhound."

"Yep." He kissed Jason's temple. "Dance with me a little more?"

"Until you're tired of it."

"Never that." He swung Mini around. His bad knee could go fuck itself.

Chapter Four

Coke and Dillon showed up early the next morning. Jason liked that they'd gotten to the hotel before the rest, giving him the lay of the land before things got serious.

He felt like he'd done pretty fucking well yesterday. He hadn't snarled at the fans in the lobby or fallen out of the elevator. Then there'd been the dancing—both the horizontal and vertical kind. That hadn't been bad at all. Jason grinned, thinking how acrobatic Bax had been feeling.

Sometimes it was worth it, renting a hotel room where the whole of the world wasn't on springs and tires.

Bax pinched his arm. "Gramps texted. Wanna go have second breakfast?" They'd had some coffee and granola bars in the room.

"Yeah. In the restaurant?" He could do coffee and a sausage biscuit pretty easy.

"Yep." Bax took his hand. "Gramps says Dillon is buying."

"Rock on." The clown made more than any of them. *Silly man.* Dillon was a good guy, though, and God knew Gramps loved the son of a bitch like no one else.

"Yeah. I like when he buys. I can get steak and eggs."

"Spoiled brat." He got his shirt tucked in, his belt fastened. "I look okay?"

"Perfect. You've always been snazzy." Bax kissed him, then mussed his hair. "Come on."

"Listen to you." Of course, that was exactly what he did these days. He listened.

"True. That's why I mussed your hair. Too perfect and folks will look harder."

"I'm fixin' to put my hat on anyway."

"Right." Bax's chuckle made him smile again. Someone just liked to fuck with him.

"Be good. So we go left out the door and down the hall a ways?"

"Yeah. I'll poke you when we're at the elevator. Count the steps?"

"Yeah." They did that, and he could remember forty-five and right. "Forty-five, man."

"Forty-five," Bax echoed. It helped to say stuff out loud.

He nodded and found the down button, tracing the braille with his fingers. He wanted to know how to do that, how to read it. He wasn't a big reader like Gramps, but he would love to be able to navigate the world better, and he missed Louis L'Amour. Surely he could learn, right? He wasn't the brightest lightning bug in the swarm, but he wasn't all that stupid.

The elevator dinged. *Slow thing.*

"You ready for this, Mini?"

"I'm ready. Let's do this thing."

Bax tugged him into the elevator, and he kept his eyes open determinedly, not wanting to get queasy.

They made it downstairs, hearing Gramps' booming voice before the doors even opened.

"—shit, Marthy! I swear to God y'all are something else. You kids best be good or I'll set Coop on you."

"Coop is like a zombie rooster," Dillon chimed in. "That's serious shit."

"True that. He's working with a broke foot and he's grumpy."

"Oh, man." Really, Coop probably needed to retire, but that wasn't his circus or his monkey. He had enough shit to worry on—whether a bullfighter retired wasn't none of his.

Coke and Dillon both called to them, and Bax took his elbow to guide him over to sit.

"Hey, y'all. How goes? Your rooms good?" Coke sounded happy, settled in his bones today.

"Yeah, it's real nice," Bax said. "What's up, Gramps?"

"Ace is going to come down for this one. Kynan's riding too. Just so you know."

"Ace Porter? What's the boss doing coming down?" Jason wasn't ready for that shit, was he?

"Who the fuck knows? I just wanted you to know."

"Dillon?" Bax sounded a little panicky. Dillon was really the brains of this operation.

"Never fear, mis amigos." Dillon's voice held laughter. "I have a plan."

"Does it involve me wearing makeup? Because if it involves me wearing makeup, I'm out."

They all cracked up, to a man.

"Hey, guys." That was AJ Gardner pulling up a chair. "What did I miss?"

"Jason in drag," Bax deadpanned.

"Huh. Nah, man. You'd look way better in a dress than Jase."

"What?" Dillon leaned forward. Jason felt the air shift. "How did I miss this?"

"Like Jason Scott would wear a dress, even as a joke." Coke's laughter boomed out. "I'm not sure he wears anything other than Wranglers and button-downs."

"True. But Bax did once. He lost a bet. That was back in our tiny tour days, right, Jase?"

"Fuck yes. He was pissed, but he didn't welch, not one bit. He came strutting out from behind the chutes, and the clown—I don't even remember his name no more—damn near swallowed his tongue." Jason felt the laughter just trying to bubble over.

Bax snorted. "At least I didn't have to wear high heels. I woulda killed myself."

"Missy puts them things on for church. One day she's gonna go ass over teakettle."

Coke's chuckled sounded fond to him. "Oh, Aje, girls are good at that shit."

"Spoken like a man." That voice was female, and not Missy at all. Did he know that voice?

"Oh, my best girl!" Dillon sounded over the moon, damn near tripping over his boots.

"Hey, clown." There was a great scraping of chairs, so Jason stood, figuring that was what cowboys did for a lady.

"Emmy!" Even Coke was tickled. "Hey, girl. Have you met Jason Scott and Andy Baxter?"

"I haven't. I know all about y'all, of course. I'm tickled shitless to meet you." Emmy took his hand, the motion easy as anything. "Mr. Scott. Emmy Sayer."

"Pleased to meet you, ma'am."

"Jase, this is Cotton's wife. She's the lady in charge of communications for Ace."

"Oh, you're the new webmaster, huh?" Bax liked the new website.

"Among other things." She chuckled. "May I sit?"

"Absolutely." Dillon was up to something. Jason could hear it.

"Thanks. Man, I could use a cup of coffee." A chair scraped back. "Thanks, Dil."

"You're more than welcome, honey." He could hear everyone pulling in tighter, drawing together.

That meant it was time to lower voices and have a come-to-Jesus moment. Bax was right there, right next to him, and he was fucking grateful for it. He needed to know that Bax was watching while he listened. Together they figured shit out but good. Separately, they were the kings of fucked-up-ness. That had always been the way, even before they were what they were now.

"Okay, so." That was Emmy, and she sounded all business. "Dillon asked me to get a few things going."

"Like what?" Bax asked.

"Earpieces. Dil's going to be the dude who's wired up, at least in the big show, but he'll be able to give Jason here clear direction."

"Why Dillon? Wouldn't Bax be the smarter choice?" Jason asked.

"Bax is going to have to do his job up on the chutes. Dillon's mic is off during the rides and he's used to flipping back and forth. Andy will have to learn for the little shows, but you're going to have to announce your intentions soon." Gramps sounded worried, so he'd been hearing the same rumbles that Jason had.

Fuck a doodle do.

Jason swallowed hard. "I been winning too much to stay down. People are jawing."

"You know it. We do this, we do it big and we take the whole purse."

"You say 'we' like Jase has a mouse in his pocket, Gramps." AJ sighed. "I mean, y'all know I got your back, but there's gonna be hell to pay from the big guys. I got the ranch, but what about you, Dillweed? Emmy, you work for the lot of them. You talked to Cotton about this?"

"I have. He's got a couple of good bloodlines going at the ranch. We're good." Emmy said it firmly. Solid.

Dillon snorted. "I have an ironclad contract, boys. If they break it, they owe me more than they pay me annually. I make a hell of a lot of money."

"Gramps?"

"You couldn't get rid of my happy ass, son. I'm in, all the way."

Jason sat there, about as numb and honored as a blind man could be.

Bax laughed, the sound suspiciously watery. "Is this gonna distract Jase? I mean, what if Dillon shouts and he jumps off or something?"

Dillon tsked. "Have some faith. I know when to shut up."

"We'll have to practice some. That's this weekend, huh?" He swallowed hard, but he was willing and at least reasonably able.

"It is." Someone touched his hand. He thought it was Emmy. "We'll do a dry run here at the hotel. All clandestine and spy-like." She giggled softly. "I rented us a conference room. Told them we were having a team-building exercise."

"You're evil, Em. I like it." Dillon slapped the table. "When is Nattie in, Coke? We need him."

"He'll be here around noon. He's picking up tacos."

"Good man." Tacos made every adventure easier.

"Mmm. Tacos." Bax hummed. *Always thinking with his stomach.*

"So, we'll meet in the conference room about noon, and we'll work this out. The boss doesn't show until tomorrow morning. It's his lady's birthday and they're having a 'spa day'." Emmy couldn't have sounded more wicked.

"Oh, man, someone needs to get pictures." Dillon was positively gleeful.

Jason wasn't a hundred percent sure he knew what a spa day was, but he knew that he didn't want one, not with that tone of voice.

"Yep." Emmy had a great laugh, kinda throaty and deep. "Okay, we'll mobilize after tacos. Save me two chicken."

"Bawk, bawk." Dillon was a dork.

"Oh, I'll show you clucking." The sound of a scuffle started up, ending abruptly when he heard Cotton shout, "Hey, that's my wife!"

And didn't the little redhead sound tickled as fuck about that fact, still?

"Lord, what a ship of fools," AJ said. Man, he sure was down.

"What's up, Aje? It cain't just be all this with me." Jason knew AJ too well.

"I'm just tired, man. Tired of the game, and Benji's not...well, he's not getting any better, and I got the new babies at home. It ain't fun no more. I have somewhere else to be."

"So, retire. God knows you got enough work on the ranch." AJ's people had a ton of land.

"Yeah. I'm… I'm in for you, buddy. Then I'm gone."

"Oh, Aje." He reached out with one hand, and AJ grabbed it, just squeezing. "Thank you."

"You guys know I would never let you down."

Bax snorted. "Unless you cook."

"Fuck you, Andy."

"That's Jason's job." There was a second of silence at Dillon's words, then the wild laughter rang out.

He could only imagine the stares and smiles that would draw. The laughter, not the other. There were always fans sitting around watching.

"Come on, y'all. We'll go have a cup of coffee at the Denny's. It's across the parking lot." Coke stood and stretched, the soft moan pained.

"Sure. You okay, Gramps?" He kept his voice low, but that groan worried him a bit.

"Fine as frog hair."

"He pulled a groin in Decatur."

Dillon was always willing to tell on Coke.

"Then he'll have to be careful here," Bax said. Jason could imagine the stern stare.

"Y'all don't worry on this old man. I'm on it."

"You always are, Hoss. Where are y'all headed?" Nate's voice hit him at the same moment as the smell of tacos. "I brought the food."

"You're early, bud," Coke shot back. "We were heading to get coffee."

"They got that Starbucks thing in the lobby," Nate said. "Dillweed?"

"Right. Coffee for all. Lay it on me." Dillon could rattle off a coffee order a mile long without blinking.

Emmy squealed. "Venti light mocha Frappuccino with two extra shots and no whip!"

"Done. Drip coffee for Coke, Nattie and AJ. Jason?"

"I want one of the vanilla milkshake deals, please."

"Big or small? Andy?"

Bax answered. "He wants the medium one. I'll take a venti mocha with double whip."

"Cotton wants a grande latte with a shot of hazelnut, please, Dill."

"Rock on, Em." He heard Dillon's whistle disappear.

"Well, then, we ought to find us a more private place to sit." Nate sounded a little wore.

"Miss Emily got us a conference room," Jason said, and suddenly everyone was moving, Bax right there at his elbow.

The heavy tread of cowboy boots on tile, then carpet, made him smile. *A herd of turtles, this bunch.*

Still, they were herding for him, and he knew it. They were all counting on his skinny ass to make this work. *No pressure there.* Then again, nothing about his fucking job had ever been easy, and now he had Bax. Had him in every way.

He was a bull rider. He'd been born a bull rider and he'd never be anything else, so he'd better take it while he could.

"Mmm. God those tacos smell good." Bax guided him to a chair, and he heard paper crinkling. "You want salsa, Mini?"

"Yeah, please."

"So, catch me up," Nate said, and one big hand caught Jason's, guiding him to the pack of three tacos.

"Emmy has an earpiece for me and Dillon will call the shots. So far that's it."

"So they calling you up to the big show?"

"Ace asked damn near a month ago," Bax murmured.

"We're fixin' to practice. Maybe I can ride around on the rolling chair." He rolled his eyes.

"Very funny. Maybe you can ride Nate." Bax was getting snarly.

"Nah, I'm wore out. You know they got me doing that microphone thing for the televised show, right?"

"Shit. Yeah, you'll have to be careful, Nattie." Coke chuckled. "Not that you ain't always."

He closed his eyes and focused on the food. He was already fucking tired.

Bax touched his wrist. "Sorry, Mini. I think I need food."

"It's all good. Tacos, then I'll figure this out."

"We will. We got tons of help." Bax chuckled low.

A fuck ton, even. "Yessir."

"It will be easier. You have someone to tell you. I won't have to shout so much."

Not that Bax couldn't holler. *Lord have mercy*.

He grabbed a taco, knowing Bax had put salsa on. He could smell it.

Time to eat, then learn this new thing Dillon had dreamed up.

Seemed like all he did these days was learn shit.

It really did make a man tired.

* * * *

"All right. Head down the center aisle, Jason. Two steps to your right, then straight on." Dillon gave Jason directions like he'd been born to it. Boom. He could tell Jase exactly what he needed to do in as few words as possible.

It was kinda magical.

It sorta pissed Bax right the hell off, too. Seriously, how did it come so fucking easy to the clown? He and Mini, they could try for an hour and all they'd end up doing was snarling.

"Good. Now turn right. Right. Now!"

Jason turned, his eyes searching for something to land on.

"Now, run." Dillon wasn't letting up on Mini at all. Not one bit.

Jason took off and Gramps caught him right before he hit the wall. "Gotcha."

A bark of laughter burst from Jason. "Sure, but this ain't real."

Emmy snorted. "Then let's take it to the hall, gents."

"What? No." No, his Mini wasn't going to be running around like a fool in public.

"No drills," Dillon said. "Just direction. I'll go ahead and tell him who all is coming."

"Okay." But he was staying right there.

"I'll take the back and keep folks from sneaking up," Coke said.

"I think Gramps needs to rest," Bax whispered to Jason. The old man was looking peaked and rough around the edges.

"We can break it up if we need to."

"Dillon seems to think you need more training."

Bax sighed and nodded. Coke Pharris would do what he would, and damn the torpedoes. The man was a force of nature, and his man Dillon was a freaking machine.

He was pretty sure he wasn't. He just felt worried and tired.

Jason touched his hand. "Let's go."

"I got you." Always.

"I know." And that was that.

They all moved out into the hall, and Bax felt like they were in some movie about really stupid spies. Seriously, anyone would take one look at them and know they was up to something.

Of course, Dillon looked confident, sure, like they weren't trying to pull the wool over everyone's eyes. That Emmy lady, she was something else too. She didn't look a bit guilty. Mini looked worried and Coke looked tired. Bax didn't know what the hell to do…

"Ace! Ace is coming. Go go go." Dillon's voice came through the earpiece loud enough that Bax heard him.

"Come on, Mini." Back to the conference room, close the door. Bax took Jason's arm and Jason turned with him easily.

"Was that real, Bax?"

"I think so, but Dillon was out of sight at that point."

"Well, one way or the other." Jason leaned against the door. "Is this gonna work, Bax?"

"It is. You got this. Hell, Dillweed can remind you to keep your eyes open."

"Shut up." Oh, that made Mini grin.

"Make me." He yanked Jason up against him, needing a kiss. Right now. Jason gave it up, easy as pie, smashing their lips together with a hum. Bax held on, all his worry dissipating with that contact. When Mini touched him like that, all was right with the world. This was his one true thing.

Mini leaned on him. "My head hurts, Bax."

"Then you need a nap. Maybe a Coke." He slipped off the earpiece Jason wore. "No more games today."

"No. No more." There was a loss, an exhaustion in those always-searching eyes.

"Come on." He would find someone to give the tech to, and he and Mini would get some quiet time.

They could rest together, cover Mini's eyes. Have an Advil, because Bax's head was starting to pound.

It was Nate they ran into. "Y'all disappeared."

"Yeah. Jase is beat. We're going to the room for a bit."

Nate opened his mouth to protest, but Bax just shook his head. He handed Nate the earbud. "We'll give it another go tomorrow before the rest of the riders get to the arena."

"I can do it tomorrow." Jase was white as a sheet.

"Okay." Nate gave Bax a sad look. "No problem, guys. You go on."

Bax wanted to scream at them. No one got to feel sorry for Jase. Mini was the best of all of them.

Instead, he took Jason's elbow and left. They needed space.

Funny, isn't it? How spaces are getting smaller and smaller?

"Thanks, Bax." Jason said it quiet, soft.

"Sure. I want you to come and lay down with a rag over your eyes, okay?" They had to hurt so bad.

"Yes, please." Once they were in the elevator, Jase moved into his arms, leaning on him.

"Soon." He'd turn off the phones and order up a pizza later tonight.

"Mmm. Feels better already."

"It does, Mini. It so does." He hugged Jason tight, not willing to let go, not even when the doors opened. Lucky for them, no one was there. One of these days, he was going to get them in trouble.

They hit the room, and he got Jason stretched out, boots off. "I'll get that washcloth."

"Thank you."

"I know it has to help."

"It does. It just makes everything less throbby."

He believed it. Jason was always trying to see, fighting to make things make sense. The docs all said that was because his eyes still worked. It was his brain that didn't process things no more. Still, he loved the way that just covering them could relax Jase to the bone.

The washcloths were nice and soft, so he wet one, then squeezed out the excess water. Bax took it back, sitting on the bed next to Jason. "Close your eyes, babe. I'm going to make it better."

"Please."

The washcloth folded, he placed it over Jason's eyes, and his Mini relaxed, a soft sigh sounding. "There you go."

He stroked Jason's forehead. The first time he'd done this, he'd felt like all sorts of a girl, petting Jase's head, but it had done wonders, so he kept it up.

"Mmm." Jason's happy little rumble kept him planted right where he was, touching, easing that pain. "I want to do this right, Bax, for us."

"I know you do." He took Jason's hand with his free one. "You need to hear this from me right now. Ain't no way you can do it wrong. You tell me today, right now, you want to quit and go do underwater basket weaving for a living? I'm with you."

"I want to win the title, then retire. I want to learn to read and stuff so I can do better, but I got to do this first."

"Then we do it." He stroked the want line that had appeared on Jason's forehead above the cloth.

Jason smiled, the look vaguely wondering. "Love the way that feels, man."

"Good. I like doing it for you." Bax hated how little he could do, but this made him feel useful.

"You do everything. I worry that my burden's too big."

"Shit, Mini. We're just trying to make it through the day." *We're both idiots, huh?*

"No shit on that. I give thanks every day we wake up and we ain't killed something."

"Right?" He had to laugh at that. He wondered if everyone who got real hurt doing what they did felt that way. Coke. Sam Bell. It had to be the same, kinda.

The game changed them all, mostly for the worse, he thought. Still, they loved it and they played it, damn the consequences. It was an addiction no cowboy could shake once it took hold.

Bax finally kicked off his boots so he could settle next to Mini on the bed. His leg ached, and he wondered if there was rain in the forecast.

Jason reached over, rubbing the sore spot unerringly, just like he felt it too.

"Mmm." Oh, that was fine. Damned fine. "Thanks."

"Anytime. We're going to do this, right? You and me? Like after?"

"Yes. You and me. Always." He wouldn't leave Jason for anything. He would figure out how to get him help. A dog. Braille lessons.

"Okay. I can do this, but I want you with me."

"I'm not goin' nowhere. I swear."

"I bet we go lots of places. Hell, I'm prob'ly the most traveled not-supposed-to-be-blind guy on earth."

"I bet you are." God, Mini still made him laugh like a loon.

Jason's laughter joined up with his and he thought, maybe, this was gonna be fine. Maybe.

He would just close his eyes and pray. That usually worked for him.

Chapter Five

The crowd was buzzing, loud enough that Jason felt a little dizzy, but Dillon was in his ear, calm and solid. The man wasn't working the event, so he could sit and talk without all the heavy breathing and screaming into the mic that came with being a rodeo clown.

"How come Dillon don't look crazy talking to himself, Bax?"

There was a hesitation, then a chuckle. "He got his phone out. Looks like he's talking on it. Not bad, for a geek from Idaho."

"Cool." Jason had pulled Bogbaby today, who was rank enough, he guessed, especially for where he'd landed on the roster. The bull was a strong son of a bitch that spun toward the right and kicked like a balky mule. Jason could make some money on the ride, if he stuck.

"Yeah. He's smarter than he looks under all that makeup."

"That he is." Hell, Gramps liked him. That was good enough for Jason. Dillon had always had his back, so Jason wasn't going to make fun of him too much.

"Keep your eyes open," Gramps told him.

"I will."

"I mean it, son. Ace is watching." That deep voice sounded so damn dire in warning.

"No pressure."

"None at all."

"You ready, Mini? Your bull is roped and in the chute." Bax was right there. Always. Solid as a rock, and never letting him get too nervous.

"I'm ready." He moved like he knew what he was doing, which he reckoned he did, when it got right down to it. Riding bulls was in his genes and in his muscle memory. His eyes didn't have to help.

He swung over the gate, focusing on the rhythm of rope and glove, of getting his legs down between bull and chute and not getting them too bad squashed. Jason took a deep breath, and he could hear both Bax and Dillon talking.

Dillon murmured. "Okay. Coke took lead, so he'll be the closest of the bullfighters. Listen to him when he gives you direction."

Right. He closed his fist around the rope, pounding his fingers closed with his free hand. *This one spins toward the right. Remember. Toward the right.*

"Head up, eyes on the prize," Bax called out.

"Yeah, yeah." Jason had this. He did. He felt as soon as he was in the middle, and he nodded just like he always did, with his eyes wide open. *Bring it on.*

Bogbaby spun out, the bull leaping out of the gate, heels snapping up as he bucked. He cleared the gate, because there was no jolt of hooves hitting metal, then turned back to the right. Spinning and kicking, just like Jason remembered, like Coke and Dillon had drilled into him. Predictable bulls were good.

He forced his eyes open, his free arm up as he spun. *Four. Five. Six.*

He began to slide to the right, but he kicked out with his right leg, pushing back up until his ass was in the middle like his mind was already. Mind in the middle, and that was half the battle. All bull riders knew that.

"You got this, Jase! Spur! Spur!" Bax was shouting like he always did, too, probably jumping and pounding the rail.

Jason spurred. He trusted Bax with his life and he had to believe it was safe to let it all hang out for the extra points.

The buzzer sounded and he jumped off, hearing Dillon in his ear. "Right! Right!"

He ran right, feeling the hot blow of the bull's breath on his neck. Coke grabbed him and tossed, and he was flying toward the fence.

He staggered, hands out, and Dillon barked, "Ace!" in his ear just as strong hands caught him and helped him up the fence. "You all right, Jason?"

"Right as rain, Ace!" He grinned as wide as he could. "Not a bad ride, huh?"

"Good one, cowboy." Ace twirled him away, he assumed toward the gate, so he put his head down to walk, avoiding the camera.

"Head up, Jase. To the right. A little more. A little more."

He kept moving right.

And there he was, out of the gate with Bax meeting him, taking his arm. He could breathe a sigh of relief. He headed right to the chutes, letting himself be led to his pocket of friends.

"Good ride," AJ told him, clapping him on his back.

"Thanks. Score?"

"Eighty-seven." Bax sounded tickled as shit.

"Woo." That meant he'd have to ride in the short go, he'd bet. That was both too cool and terrifying.

"Yeah. You'll have one more ride today." He wasn't sure Bax sounded all that happy about that.

"I can do it." Jason barely even felt queasy.

"Good job, kiddo," Dillon said in his ear. "Cameras coming."

He pulled his hat down and went for his trademark scowl.

"So sexy." Dillon was cruising for a bruising.

"Jason! Jason, are you back for real? Your fans are asking." Whoever that was had a chirpy damn voice.

"I am. Working my way to the big show." *Fucker.*

"We're all waiting to see that." The lady just went on and on, but he was known for ignoring the non-arena announcers. TV had never been his forte.

"You and me both," Bax muttered.

"Shh." Jason had to smile, though. It was actually easier to hide at the big events.

The crowd noises rose and fell, then went quiet.

Damn, someone got hurt.

He shook his head, not wanting to know, really. He had to, but he didn't want to.

"Come on, Mini. Let's get a water before they call you up. You're going to be the leader going into the short go."

"Who got hurt?"

"Houston again. Damn kid needs to get his mind in the middle."

Jason shook his head. "He wouldn't know what to do iff'n his bell wasn't rung."

"I guess so." Bax chuckled, leading him around behind the chutes.

"I did okay?" he whispered.

"Shit, you looked Ace right in the eye and smiled. I damn near swallowed my teeth."

"Good deal. I was going for it, you know?"

"You were. This is your season, Mini." Was that Bax's hand on his ass?

"It better be, huh?" He flexed. *Yeah. Hand. Ass. In public.* His cheeks heated but he couldn't stop grinning.

"No one's watching, Mini. You're good."

"I am. You're crazy."

"Yeah. It feels cool to be a little crazy sometimes."

"It does." He was getting ready to let things ease up, if he were honest.

Bax led him to a chute, and he grasped the rail. *Nothing to do now but wait.* "You hungry?"

"Nah. We'll order pizza at the hotel." Sharing a pizza with Andy Baxter was one of his oldest things. His dearest.

"Cool. The corny dogs here smell like ass."

"So long as they still look like dicks, right?"

Bax hooted like a big old owl. "Well, if you're eatin' 'em, yeah."

"I'd rather have the real deal," he muttered.

"I know. You win big and buy the pizza and I'm all yours."

"Heads up," Dillon said in his ear. "You pulled Bogie for the short go."

"Rock on. Time to go do my thing again, then pizza and blow jobs."

Bax laughed right out loud, and he could imagine the guys grinning along and having no idea. No one knew how sexual his Bax really was. No one but him. *Thank God for that.* "Gonna embarrass myself, Mini. You behave."

"I don't know what you're on about. Not at all."

"Mmm. Evil man. Okay, we're loaded. We'll go after Dale Loomis."

"I'm the only one who rode in the main round?"

"Yeah. It was a bad night."

"Shit." All eyes would be on him.

"You're in the money, no matter what. Just stick."

Right. Just stick. Mind in the middle. Keep your fucking eyes open.

He climbed the rail under Bax's urging. He loaded up, breathing deep and rocking back and forth to make room for his leg.

"You need the 4x4, Mini?"

Jason nodded to Bax. "Son of a bitch is trying to squat on me."

"Got it. Gramps. He's getting too low."

"Come on, you old bitch. Get your happy ass up." Coke's voice was rough as a cob and familiar as breathing.

He knew instantly the bull would behave for Coke. It was insane, but the world listened to his oldest friend.

The bull stood up, so Jason nodded, wanting out of the chute before it all went south. This little bull was an easy ride, if he just kept his mind in the middle. He would spin, kick, then let the rider off real nice. Job done.

Up. Down. Up. Down. And in the money. *Bingo.*

He hit the ground, and Dillon was calm this time. "He's out already. Just head left."

"Got it," he muttered. He walked careful, giving a two-fingered salute to the crowd.

"Good boy. They'll want you for the check thing. Get your sunglasses."

"Not a boy, fucker." He pushed his hat down lower and took his bull rope and glasses from Coke. "Thanks."

"No prob. Cricket will walk you up."

"Good deal. Big big check or no?"

"Nope. Check, buckle."

"Ah." He would hold up the buckle and wee check and smile.

It was over quickly, and he was moving toward Bax's voice, trying his best not to stumble.

"Hey, champ." For a moment he couldn't place the voice, but then he knew it was Raul, the Brazilian he barely knew. One warm hand grasped his elbow. "They tell me change in light makes you dizzy. You go this way."

"Thanks, buddy. It's maddening, no shit. Didn't know you were here."

"Came in second. Beat your ride in the short go."

But I took the event, didn't I? "I been in my own little world."

"Mmm-hmm. Here is Andy."

"Thank you, buddy."

"Of course. I have your front."

Jason chuckled softly. Raul's English was getting better, but sayings were hard. "Your back."

"Sim. Your back." Raul clapped him on the shoulder before walking off.

"So all the Brazilians know?" Jason asked.

Bax snorted. "Balta knows. So do Joa and Raul."

"True that. Balta had to know, right?"

"No shit. Balta would get his panties in a wad if he was left out." Bax sighed, but Jason thought he was grinning.

"I did good." He let the pleasure in that wash over him.

"You did more than good, Mini. You won."

"I did. I got my invite to the big show, Bax. I did it." He was scared to death. But this was the deal, right? He could be scared, but he couldn't be a coward. He had to win this shit so he could have the time and money to figure out how to be blind. He wanted to make it work, needed to.

Bax deserved someone who could pull his own weight when they retired. He deserved to fucking be that someone. Somehow.

"You okay?" Bax asked. "I got your go bag."

"I am. I'm good. Proud." And that was the truth.

Bax's fingers closed around his wrist, squeezing. "You're amazing."

"I'm yours. Pizza."

"Blow jobs," Bax whispered.

"God yes. Please." He couldn't stop grinning.

"Soon." Bax led him past a crowd of folks and he nodded and smiled, trusting his glasses to hide all.

Bax got him loaded into the truck, the sudden silence a touch overwhelming. Jason looked around wildly, trying to see anything, but Bax caught his hand, distracting him.

"Hey. Sorry. I just… Sorry."

"No big, Mini. I'm starting to figure out shit."

"Yeah?"

"Yeah." Bax sounded pleased with himself. Really pleased. "I can tell, you know? When you're overwhelmed."

Jason wasn't totally sure if that was good or bad. "I'm sorry. I don't mean to be."

"Hell, I know that, doof." Bax got the truck rolling. "It can't be easy."

He didn't know. It was what it was. He was fucking tickled that Bax put up with him.

"So, what are we getting on the pizza tonight?" Bax asked, sounding like he couldn't be more tickled.

"Pepperoni and sausage and onions."

"Onions burn."

He burst out laughing. Someone was way more focused on the blow job than the pizza. "Green peppers?"

"They make you burp."

"Jalapenos."

Bax whacked his leg.

"All meat, and we get our blow jobs while we're waiting." He knew that was a great compromise.

"That's perfect." Bax laughed with him now.

"I'm on a motherfucking roll, cowboy."

"You so are, Mini. Good thing I'm riding with you."

"No shit on that."

They pulled up at the hotel in no time, the engine dying off under Bax's hand. "Come on, Mini. We got a date."

"Yessir. I'm all in." In fact, he might even be deeper than that.

Bax made him feel ten feet tall and stronger than the mountains. Winning didn't hurt that feeling, either.

Chapter Six

"AJ! You got any Cokes?" Bax loved AJ's ranch. Even with all the kids and other assorted family members, it was a comfortable place, and the guest house was real nice. A break from hotels and RV living.

"In the fridge." AJ was braiding one of the little girls' hair, his fingers surprisingly nimble.

"Cool." Andy grinned, making his way to the fridge. He was dry as a bone.

The house was full of family, just like always, and he welcomed the noise, the distractions. They were fixin' to have to talk about the big leagues, and Andy had to admit, he was worried. Their plan had worked so far, but what if that was a fluke? What if…the bulls on the big show were twenty times more powerful, the guys more competitive, the cameras—

This couldn't work.

He popped the top on his Coke, then took a long swig. Oh, that burned good. There was nothing like that, nothing.

Coke came wandering in, nodding to him.

"Gramps? What the hell are you doing here?"

"Came to talk to Jason on my way home. AJ says there's Cokes?"

"In the fridge." He rolled the bottle against his neck. "Mexican Coke, even."

"Any Dr Pepper?"

"Here, Unca Poppy." Benji trotted to the fridge, AJ's oldest always willing to help Coke out.

"Thank you, son. You are a good kid." Coke smiled at Benji and took the can with a smile.

"I try." Benji gave Coke an adoring smile, and Coke ruffled the kid's hair.

"You doing okay, Andy? You look pinched."

Bax spread his hands, looking for answers. "How are we gonna do this, Gramps? I 'bout died when Ace caught Jason up at the show."

"We're gonna brazen it out like the whores we are. I can't think of anything else to do."

Bax chuckled. "I guess so. Lord, lord."

Gramps winked at him. "What's the worst thing that could happen?"

"Uh, we could get sued."

"For what? No one's asked us if he was blind."

"No, but ain't we endangering—"

"Who? All us bullfighters and the gate pullers are in on it." Coke snorted. "Jason ain't being forced. What they gonna do?"

"I dunno. I'm scared he'll get hurt again." There it was. The worst that could happen.

"He could."

And that was that, right? It was what their kind did, got hurt.

Coke shrugged. "He needs this, son."

"I know. I'm hanging on, Gramps."

"That's all we can do. We got to make this happen. Jase is getting twitchy."

"He is," Bax agreed. "He's wanting to get on to the realities of his life."

"Then we finish this Chapter up."

"Right." He grabbed Gramps' arm. "Thanks. I mean it."

"Sure, Andy. We'll manage. Where's Jase?"

"Sitting in the quiet." The kids could wig Jason out fast. All but Benji. Mini loved that little boy and had the patience of a saint with him. It was bizarre.

"Unca Jason?" Benji clapped his hands. "I'll take him a Coke."

"He would love that, I bet." Jason would never send Benj away.

"Okay. I'll be careful." Benji pulled out another Dr Pepper and walked off, his face a study in concentration.

Coke watched Benji with a soft smile, then turned to Andy. "Once it comes out, it'll fall apart fast, but until that happens, we just keep praying."

"Got it." God knew he could pray. He had Jason-shaped calluses on his knees.

"You two look too serious, eh?" Dillon came bebopping over.

"Do I?" Coke wrapped one hand around Dillon's waist.

"You do." Dillon beamed, then nodded at him. "Jason did good at the event. I was pleased. He's smarter than he looks."

Bax snorted. "He's smarter than me, for sure."

"I ain't smarter than no one," Coke hummed, and the sound was familiar. Solid.

Dillon dug into Coke's ribs. "You're just as smart as you need to be."

"You're Coke Pharris. You just are, man." No one would ever be Gramps. No one.

Coke chuckled. "Whatever that means. Okay, y'all get rest tonight. We'll talk in the morning."

"Sure. Sure, you going to hang out then?"

"We're going to pick up a bill of groceries. I'll get a couple briskets."

"Ooooeee." He made the Beau Lafitte noise, just because that was what Beau would say to brisket.

"Very nice. Y'all have something for supper?"

"Uh." They probably had a box of mac and cheese.

"You want we should grab y'all tacos and drop 'em off?"

"Thank you. That would be great, man." He handed Coke a few bills. "Can you bring us some Cokes?"

"What kind? Dr Pepper?"

"Yeah."

"Got it." Dillon plucked the money from Coke's hand. "We'll be back."

"Good deal. I appreciate it." He headed off, hunting his man. He found Jason on the back porch in a rocker, Benji in his lap, along with the twins in a carrier at his feet.

"Hey, you," Jason said softly.

"Heard me coming, huh?"

"Always."

The single word made the pit of his belly ache.

"You got roped into babysitting?"

"I told them I'd sit here while they were changing the babies' beds and stuff. Apparently there was drama."

"Ah." He sank down in a chair next to Mini. "Coke and Dill are getting tacos."

"Rock on. Crispy beef?"

"No, soft chicken," he teased. "You know I got your back."

"You do. You so do." Jason grinned at him. "I got me a Benji."

"He's pooped, huh? All the excitement." Poor kid tired out fast—maybe faster than he used to.

"I guess? He might be getting a cold. He has a little wheeze."

"Aw, man. You better tell Missy." With Benj, colds could be bad.

"Yeah, when I see her." Jason grinned in his direction again, looking happy as a pig in slop.

"Ha ha. You're so funny." He did laugh, though, because he had to. "Coke wants to powwow in the a.m., but he's giving us tonight off."

"Well, thank God for favors, large and small."

Ooh, Mini was a little snippy now.

"You want me to tell him no?" Bax would, even if they did need to strategize.

"No. No, I just… I'm just being a bitch. No worries."

"You know I will. Hell, Dillon might call it off for a few days. Gramps is tired." Bax could see it in every inch of the man. The weight of the world was on him.

"We'll see. Dill is good for him. Keeps him in line." Jason rocked Benji slowly.

Bax sat on the porch steps, looking at the babies. "You ever want any?"

"Any what? Clowns?"

"No. God. Kids, Mini. Did you ever think on it?"

Jason shook his head. "Nope. I only ever thought about you."

He had to smile at that. "Took us long enough."

"It did. Took me damn near dying."

He reached over to put his hand on Jason's arm. "We had shit timing, but I got you now." They had this conversation a lot, but he wasn't gonna complain. They both needed reassurance right now.

"And you're fixin' to keep me."

"I so am. You think you'll get a dog?" He meant a seeing-eye one, but kept it neutral in case someone was nearby.

"I think so. I want to. I want to be useful, you know? I mean, shit, Bax. I ain't got no skills."

"Sure you do, Mini." Most of them required a man to see, but they had people to help teach Jason. Bax had looked it up online.

"You heard of many blind ranchers?"

"Nope, but that don't mean nothin'. People lie all the time."

"True, that. We'll reckon it, one way or the 'tother."

"We always do." Lovers or not, they'd been two heads better than one for years. Neither one of them was worth a plug nickel alone.

Jason beamed at him. "Yessir, we do."

Benji stirred. "Unca Jason? Did I sleeps on you?"

"You did, man! We napped together."

"Oh, good! Momma might yell, though. Naps this late make me stay up."

Jason chuckled softly and hugged Benji. "I won't tell if you won't."

"Okay. Are you hungry? I saved you a bag of Ruffles."

"You know how I feel about my chips, little man."

"I'll go get them!" Benji eased off Jason's lap. He was always so careful.

"Lord have mercy. The babies okay, Bax?"

"Sleeping the sleep of the righteous."

"What do they look like?"

"Babies."

"Bax!" Jason laughed, though, and he didn't elaborate, because it was true. They were baby-shaped. Babies all looked like soft old men without the wrinkles. It was weird.

AJ came out with a grin. "Y'all rock. Thank you for watching them."

"Hey, no problem. Not like they could crawl away." Bax chuckled at Jason's words.

"Soon. So damn soon." AJ sighed. "They might not be able to say what they need, but man, they're not mobile. So much easier."

"You have to be used to it now, though. Right?"

"Practiced, yeah. Used to? No. The new ones always have something to teach you, I promise."

"Huh. Like dogs or horses?" Bax could see that. All baby animals had to be the same, right?

"Andy Baxter, my babies are not like horses." Missy's lips were tight, and she was glaring, but he thought she was playing.

"Oh, I dunno. They get to where they run around like foals eventually." He winked at her through the gloom.

"Butthead men. Thanks for watching the babies, Jase. I appreciate it."

"Anytime, Missy. They just sat there."

"Still did me a world of good. You two hanging out until Fearless returns with the tacos?"

"We're gonna go to the house and rest. I need a shower." Jase stood, sounding sure as shit.

Bax rose as well. "Thanks for letting us stay, huh?"

Missy snorted and waved them off while AJ chuckled. "See you tomorrow."

Jason knew the way, picking along steadily, and no one would know in the half-light that he wasn't just being careful not to trip.

Pride swelled in Bax's chest. Jason was a freakin' miracle. He really was.

"So…you really want a nap?" he asked.

"Nope."

"A shower?" Bax needed a roadmap here.

"Mmhmm." Oh. Oh, okay. That was a hungry little sound…

Shower together then. With benefits. *Woohoo.*

He stepped a little closer, wanting to see the half smile he knew was on Mini's face. "I might be a little dirty myself."

"Only a little?"

"Well, you know, how are you gonna see the dirt?" Bax looped an arm around that lean waist.

"I'm willing to scrub you down, check you out, up close."

"Maybe make sure I smell good?" God, he loved this game.

"Make sure you taste right."

Oh fuck. His body tightened, his cock giving a little jerk of happiness. They both moved faster, stumbling to the guest house, which was huge compared to their trailer or a hotel. "In, Mini. I want you."

"Do you?" Jason pulled him in then pushed him up against the door with a *thud.*

"Fuck, yes. You make me nuts." They were catching up on all that lost time. That was the only explanation for the constant fire Jason lit in his belly.

"Good. I want you to ache for it."

"Feel." He pressed up against Jason, arching so that Jase felt him through their jeans, hard and ready.

"Man..." Jason knelt, just slid along his body, easy as pie. "Gimme."

"Okay." Bax undid his buckle and button, then eased open his zipper.

He stared down, his eyes burning in his skull as those lips popped open for him. Jason took him in, licking at the head of his cock, making his toes curl inside his boots.

"Jesus, Mini."

"Love how you taste." The soft, maddening licks kept on and on, making his ass cheeks clench.

"Mmm. God, you feel good, Mini. So good."

He'd never believed he'd have this, that he'd know it. He'd give it up in a second for Jason to see again, but that wasn't a thing, so he was taking hold with both hands.

He stroked Jason's short hair, loving how soft it felt under his fingers. His damn hair was like a bristle brush, but Jase's was just sweet as could be. Jase moaned for him, sliding his tongue on his shaft as Jason took him in, nice and slow and sweet.

Bax panted, his belly pulling in tight. This man had an incredible effect on him. His cock was framed by his jeans, pushing out and between Jason's pink, wet lips.

That sight was enough to make a man groan. Bax shifted back and forth, his thighs like rocks. "Want you bad. I cain't... I'm fixin' to..."

Jason took him down to the root, no question. He was pretty sure Mini wasn't breathing. He arched, his back pressed to the door for leverage.

"Fuck!" He let himself scream, slamming his head back against the wood.

Jason swallowed around him, the tip of his cock pressing at the back of Jason's throat.

He was gonna lose it any damn second, and when Mini rolled his ballsac, nudging it firm enough that he swallowed, it was all over but the crying.

Bax rocked, amazed at how he'd gone from zero to sixty in just a few minutes. He was on fire, his whole body tingling. Jason's face was a study in pleasure, his eyes closed. "Hey, Mini. Come on. Bed."

"Uh-huh. You gonna love up on me?"

"I am. Make you crazy, I promise." He tugged Jason to his feet, pressing them together as they rubbed, all the way up.

"Okay. Now." Jason wrapped both arms around his neck.

"Now, Mini. Swear to God. Come to bed."

They danced, kinda. Long, short-short, all the way to the bed. Nice and easy. He kissed Jason's neck, then right up under his ear.

Jason stilled, then he shuddered. Oh, Bax loved that little hot spot. It got Mini all revved up every time. Every single time. It had taken Bax forever to find it, but now he used it with impunity.

He bit at Jason's ear, then focused back on that spot, hunting a cry.

That sound came right away. *Boom.* Jason called for him, swaying, and Bax's spent cock throbbed, wanting to go again. How could he be so damn happy and getting hard all over?

"Bax."

"I got you." He did. He would make his lover happy.

"I don't doubt you a bit." No. No, Jase believed in him like no one else, and he was fixin' to prove Jason right.

Bax took one kiss, then another, barely letting Mini breathe. He wanted Jason dazed, moaning.

He spread Jase out on the bed, arms and legs wide so he could see every inch. That lean, strong little body was way more brown now, way more like Mini. After the hospital, Jase had been pale, kind of shrunken.

Now he was hard everywhere and so fine, a line of blond hair from his belly button down led the way to glory. Bax explored, getting rid of clothes and really going to town, touching all that skin. *Hoo-yeah.* And kissing. And licking.

His need was taken care of, so he could focus on his Mini. The guy was his whole damn world. Jason was his one and only. He breathed deep, resting his cheek on Jason's belly.

"We got this, Bax. Swear to God."

"I know we do." Bax licked at Jason's skin, tasting salt.

He needed Jase to stop worrying and feel. They could obsess over everything else later. Now was for them to touch and need.

Jason reached for him, finding his head unerringly. This was where Jason was confident, knowing. He never missed.

Never.

"This is better than riding, Bax. So much better."

"Is it? I never got to tell you to keep your eyes open, do I?" No, Jase always kept them open, saying he might see Bax in his dreams. Nothing on earth had ever been so hot in the history of time.

He moaned, then licked the tip of Jase's cock, slapping it with his tongue.

"Damn! Please!" Jason sounded surprised at himself.

He chuckled, letting air flow over that hot flesh. Yeah, now he was cooking with oil. He didn't do this much—his cowboy liked sucking, liked his hand—but the cries that he was earning made him ache. Bax licked and lapped, then sucked a bit, varying the motion.

"Bax!"

He cupped Jason's balls and rolled them, and damn, but he loved that low moan. He knew his hands were rough, but Jase seemed to like it, to crave his touch, so he gave it up, no question.

"Fixin' to…" The soft warning made him smile.

"Mmmhmmm." He could take it. Hell, he was getting to be an expert. Like tapping his finger against Jason's little hole, making promises he didn't have to worry about.

He could sure enough keep them anytime with this man in his bed.

"I need…more, Bax. Please." Jase bore down, taking his finger in to the second knuckle.

"Damn. Hell, yeah. Mini. So hot inside." Bax was blown away by how Jase needed him.

Jason nodded, lips parted, tongue flicking out to wet them. He had no idea how goddamn sexy he was, but Andy Baxter knew. He was no fool. This was it for him, all the way to the bone.

This was his only thing.

He leaned forward and took a kiss, needing Mini to come on, to shoot for him, to prove how good it was.

Jason humped his hands, rocking back and forth, and devoured his mouth, really giving him what for.

When he slid his finger all the way in, curling it inside Jason's body, that was all she wrote. Jason came apart in his hands, spraying his seed.

Oh fuck, that was hot. He groaned and licked at Jase's flat belly.

"Bax! Lord have mercy." Jason clutched at him, but his hair was kinda too short to grab. "You're gonna make me… Damn."

Oh, he did like making Jase need.

He chuckled, then licked again. He wanted Jason crazy for him. Jase had started it, after all.

"You're— Damn, Bax. Come up here, you."

He climbed up Jason's body, ready for some kissing and stroking of his own. Afterglow was the best part, which he wouldn't ever have said.

Now he knew, though. Loving someone was damn cool.

Jason cradled him, dancing fingers over his skin, loving on him.

"Mmm. You feel so good, Mini."

"I feel like yours."

"You are. I got you. I keep telling you that."

Jason pinched him, not too hard, but it wasn't sweet either. "You do. Thank God for small favors. You ever—? Did you ever think on where we ought to light, after all this shit is done?"

"Huh?" He gave that the thought it deserved. "Well, Texas, broadly."

"I know that, doof." Jason sighed loud. "I was thinking about the beach, maybe. Somewhere on the Gulf."

"Yeah? I wouldn't mind the beach. I wouldn't mind that at all."

"I mean, what kind of a spread? I want a little land, you know? Room for some toys, some animals." He was grinning so hard that Jason could probably feel it.

"Sure. I can't imagine living in a condo or nothing." Jason stretched as tall as his little body allowed. "We're cowboys. We need critters and space to roam. But I want to run on the beach too."

"Sounds good. I mean, I've seen ranch-type places in Galveston." He had, right? He would google it.

Really, how hard could it be to find what they wanted? They had enough money for some acreage.

"Cool. You know I got enough to throw in with you. We could have a nice spread, some critters, dogs." Jason's smile was…blissful, like someone had given him everything he'd ever fucking wanted.

"We could." Man, his heart was just pounding suddenly. Him and Jase, they were talking forever. Oh, he knew Jase was his 'always thing', but to have it out there? "I want that."

Jase tilted his head, one hand landing like a lead balloon on his chest. "You sure, buddy? I wouldn't make you."

"Jesus, Jason. I want you, full stop. The thought of getting old with you, of getting to wake up with you every day? I couldn't ask for no more than that in any life."

He put his hand over Jase's, needing him to feel the truth.

"I'm gonna do it, Bax. I'm gonna ride in the big show and win us enough money to retire. I swear to God, I'll do it." Jase burned for him, the passion flashing in those sightless eyes.

"I believe you." It scared him to death, when Jason fell or ran the wrong way, but on sheer riding talent, he was confident that Jason could do it.

"Good, 'cause I need that. I need you, and I need to know there's something real on the other side—critters, ocean, sand, dogs, home." Jason was open to him, not blustering or hiding a bit.

"I swear it. I ain't gonna just leave."

"Me either, so we're stuck like glue."

"I love that. Love you." It still felt weird to be able to say it out loud.

Jason's face lit up in a smile, and he didn't have to hear it to know that Mini felt the same goddamn way.

Andy Baxter could see it, and he was a fucking lucky man.

Now he needed to pray that Jason was just as lucky.

Chapter Seven

Jesus, had it always been so fucking loud? Jason didn't remember the unrelenting noise at a host hotel, the press of people that never let up for a second.

And he had to start back up in Dallas, didn't he?

Damn.

Dallas was where every Tom, Dick and waiter knew bull riders by name, where fans hung out at the buffet line to try to invite the pick-up men and bullfighters to sit with them.

Bax was right there next to him, while Cotton's girl was on his other side, giggling and carrying on like a buckle bunny, all the while directing him.

Emmy was a natural wonder, with subtle arm taps and shit, and announcing each newcomer so he knew who they were and what direction to smile. "Why, Mrs. Detmiller. Nice to see you here."

He smiled and nodded, thanking the good Lord for the ten-thousandth time that he wasn't known for being friendly and chatty with the fans…just polite.

"Good ride tonight, Jason," she said.

"Thank you, ma'am."

"We need to get on," Bax murmured. "Good to see you."

He tipped his hat and they got to the elevator.

Emmy was a sweet-smelling and solid beside him, holding his arm. "I got adjoining rooms for y'all, Dillon and Gramps, me and Cotton, Nattie."

"Got us battened down, did you?" Bax sounded tickled. Jason got it. It was nice to know who was around.

"Yep. Reduce exposure, increase the joy." Emmy cackled, the sound bright and smart. Could a laugh be smart? "And you can disappear, if you need to."

"Thanks, lady. You're amazing." He stood, waiting for Bax to let him in. He did a lot of standing around.

"I try. I brought this game—you follow the sounds, follow the pattern. I know it's silly, but I love it, and it's fun. You and Andy can play for blow jobs."

"Emmy!" Bax sounded so shocked, but Jason just hooted, his shoulders coming down from around his ears.

God. God, he howled with his laughter, tickled shitless. He'd needed that, something to release the tension, ease the fear that was growing on him like kudzu on a South Carolina road.

Emmy hugged him. "I'll leave you to it. Y'all holler if you need anything. I'm on the job."

"Thank you, ma'am. We'll have a powwow tonight."

"You got it. I left your earphones here. Dillon has theirs."

"Good deal." When the door closed behind her, Jason pulled in a deep breath. "Dallas, man."

Why couldn't he have chosen an event like...hell, Mars? New Jersey? Somewhere that no one would know him but the people he needed to help him. This was like being thrown into the ocean without knowing how to swim in the lake.

"Yeah." Bax blew out a breath. "We can do this."

"We ain't got much choice, Bax."

"Nope." Bax laughed a bit. "I guess that means we've got desperation on our side."

"Well shit, we ought to be right as rain then, ain't we?" He rolled his eyes, but damn if he wasn't excited and more than ready.

They were fixin' to do this...in the big show. And he had Andy Baxter with him, all the way.

Jason groped out with one hand, and Bax took it, settling his jangling nerves in a heartbeat. "We're gonna ride, cowboy."

"If you keep your goddamn eyes open, yes."

"Shut up." He grinned, though, didn't he? His eyes were wide open right now, moving, trying to see Bax. He hated that the most, that he couldn't see that face.

"I'm right here, Mini. Stop it. I'm right here." Bax put one of Jason's hands on his face.

"I want to. I'm trying." He took one deep breath, then another. His hands mapped Bax's face, tracing the familiar shapes, giving his brain something to 'see'.

"I know. It just looks like it hurts." Bax always wanted to fix things, even his eyes.

"It's...stressful. Like there's no rest."

"Well, we'll take a few days off after, huh? Just take the travel trailer to the lake."

"Then to Oklahoma City. I want the title, Bax. I want to go out on top." He wanted the money. Now he had it in his heart, that he had a goddamn plan, he wasn't letting it go.

"We win it, then. God knows, you know how to ride."

"Yessir." He knew, dammit, and he didn't need to be all wishy-washy about it, either. It was time. He either needed to cowboy up or get back in the goddamn truck.

He nodded, because that was that, and Bax chuckled at him. "Made up your mind, have you?"

"I have. All the way."

"That makes it better." Bax lifted his hand to kiss it.

It was stupid as all get out, but true.

Now he just needed to ride like he meant it. That much he could do.

"Let's sit a minute." Bax pushed him down on the bed. "Gramps and them'll be here in a second with all advice and shit. I need to be with you a sec."

"Okay." He slid his fingers over Bax's wrist, his breath coming in sharp when Bax bent to kiss him. He did love this—more than anything, more than riding, more than life.

Bax was his damn everything.

"When you've won the championship, we're gonna buy a piece of land and settle. Have a house and shit." Bax sounded so goddamn happy.

"I'll keep telling myself this every damn day." Now that he had that goal… Well. "I want dogs."

"Anything you want."

He chuckled. 'Anything' was a big field. "Big bed?"

"Yep."

"A spider monkey?"

"Monkeys are scary, man. And dogs would eat it." Bax was laughing so hard.

"How about a lemur?" He was managing a straight face, but damn, it was taking all he had. He remembered playing with Bax, and having it back made his heart friggin' soar.

"Nah. No weird eyes. If we got to go exotic, I say llama. They kill coyotes."

"Llamas are cool." He made his eyes go wide. "Ooh. How about camels?"

"They smell bad. You remember when Gramps rode one at that fair?" Bax made a sound that Jason could so relate to the way a camel moved with someone on its back.

"Dude, that was funny as fuck. He looked uncomfortable as hell, didn't he?"

"Shit, yes. He was all worried it was gonna bite him." Bax chortled.

"Shit, you remember those huge nasty teeth?" It had been like a deformed horse's mouth or something. The teeth had looked like George Washington's dentures… "The feet were cool, though."

"And those eyelashes." Bax leaned on him, their laughter dying gently.

"So no camels, but llamas are on the table. I approve. The dogs can herd them."

"There you go." Bax fiddled with his fingers, loving on him. It wasn't perfect—he couldn't see, he was having to figure out more shit than was reasonable, and he was caught between a rock and a hard place—but goddamn, it was good.

"You want to listen to the TV, Mini? Just float together for a bit?"

"Sounds like heaven, man. We'll enjoy the calm before it comes up a storm."

Bax's chin dipped against his shoulder, letting him feel the nod. "Come on then, and settle. I got the remote." They snuggled back against the pillows, but neither one of them bothered to take off their boots.

Someone would be knocking on their door soon enough.

Someone always did.

Chapter Eight

"Okay, Jase. There's a bunch of sports reporters and photographers here today, since it's Dallas." That was Dillon, who talked a mile a minute and always knew all the angles. "If you can, head for the west gate when you come off the bull so they don't get you full in the face with pictures."

Bax didn't say nothin', just kept his head down, checking Jason's gear. Rope, gloves, vest.

"Coke will be right there, and I'll be hollering directions if you get spun and don't know west."

Jason was surprisingly relaxed, for a son of a bitch that was fixin' to ride blind at the big show. Maybe this was just his natural habitat. The little shows had been harder, less familiar. The main tour had the same arena set up as much as possible every time. Well, except for Albuquerque, which was damn small.

Dillon went on and on, a constant, steady patter that Bax was pretty sure Jase wasn't listening to. Maybe that was the point. Sam had always done that for Beau when he was pulling rope, just jabbering to keep the nerves down where they belonged.

Jase was loose, easy in his skin, breathing like he was where he needed to be.

"Keep your eyes open, Mini. You do that and you'll be fine."

Jason nodded, his jaw tight, but Bax knew that was pure concentration, not stress. Mini had his game face on.

The gate swung open, and fuck him, Mini was riding like the bull wasn't rank, like he was born to this shit. His free arm was flexible, he sat up, and at six point five seconds, damn if that man didn't start to spur.

Bax almost jumped over the rail, snatching off his hat and waving it, whooping and hollering.

Jason leapt off after the buzzer, and Dillon hollered, "Left! Left, buddy! Stop! I'm coming to shake your hand."

Jason stopped, and the moment Dillon's fingers touched his, he pulled back to run his fingers along his hat brim like he was too cool to shake the clown's hand, a joke those two had done for ages. For a long moment it was like he was back more than a year ago and nothing had changed, and Bax caught his breath.

He'd go back in a second. He'd give everything they had now away, if Mini could see.

Then Jase turned to the gate again, his head down, his jaw clenched again, just to get out of the arena, and he blew out that air, clambering down to meet his man. AJ was there, clapping Jason on the back, steering him the right way to avoid the gal with the microphone. "Good ride, man!"

"Eighty-nine-five. Not bad." Jason smiled—an actual real-life shit-eating grin, for fuck's sake. Damn.

"Not bad at all," Bax said, winking at AJ. "Come on. Let's get out of the noise, huh?" Shit, that was a hell of a good thing for the first ride back.

"Y'all ready to go?" Aje asked. "I got the truck."

"We're out." Bax grabbed their go bags. "You solid, Mini?"

"Yeah. Yeah, just let me…" Jason reached back to unhook his chaps. "Oh, damn. I think I gained weight."

"Muscles." Jason was damn near buff.

"Nah." AJ snorted at both of them. "You're frickin' tiny as ever, Mini. You're just not used to sitting in the damn chaps for three or four other riders. Small events spoil us all."

"True, that." They stomped out of the arena, avoiding the fans, the cameras and the other riders, thanks to Balta.

That Brazilian was wide, loud and sounded happy as a pig in shit running interference when Ace hollered at Jason. *Dodged that bullet, for sure.*

"I owe him one," Jase muttered. "And he'll collect. Crazy old man."

"He will. He loves being in on something." Bax had to laugh, just because it felt damn fine to be alive.

"Three more rides, then we get to go to Phoenix." Jason had this down.

"Yep. We can do this." Bax was feeling amazing. He hugged Jase as they slid into the truck.

"We will. Dammit. Pizza upstairs once the event's over, Aje?"

AJ glanced at Bax, one eyebrow up, then he grinned wide. "Hell, yeah! I'm in."

AJ loved pizza, and he would work it off. The man could gain and lose the same five pounds a million times. Mini would eat his one piece, but the invite was out there, and Jase hadn't done that in months.

God. His Mini was glowing.

Bax wanted to go two-stepping all of a sudden.

They could do it, in the suite part, just turn on some King George and go for it. Jason followed like a dream, and Bax did love to dance. After AJ left, he would make sure they rubbed belt buckles.

They ambled up to the hotel, and Aje pulled to the door. "I'm going to grab some Cokes and stuff. I'll see y'all for pizza when everyone gets here."

"Cool. See you in a bit." Bax kept it casual, but he felt like hollering, 'Score!'. He grabbed Mini by the wrist. "Come on. We're early."

"Good deal." Jason nodded, and they went in, Jase easily fielding the couple of fans who either didn't have tickets for tonight or whatever.

The confidence one ride had brought amazed him. Made him damn happy, too.

They got the elevator to themselves, and they both relaxed for the first time since they'd left the hotel.

Bax grabbed Jason's hand. "Damn good ride, Mini. Damn fine."

"It felt normal. It felt like a ride." Jason's smile was like the sun coming from behind a cloud. "I'm tired of stressing shit, Bax. I want to ride and win."

"Well, you know how to do that." He was just along for the ride. Oh, he was good enough, but he'd been injury boy from day one. Mini was a master class on how to get it done.

"I do." Jason yelped when Bax dragged him out of the elevator and down the hall. He wanted to beat the crowds. Jason could run, though, and he didn't question Bax, just came along, sweet as you please.

He got them into the room. "Stay right there." He didn't worry about the arena dust. He just plugged his phone in before calling up his favorite playlist.

"Bax?" Mini tilted his head, curious.

"Hear that King George?" Now that was a boot-sliding song. He moved close again to take Jason in his arms.

"Oh." Mini relaxed. "I do. I hear you, Bax."

"Mmmhmm. You know I like a victory dance." He used to have to dance with any girl who was willing but not clingy. Now he had this man to touch and hold.

He thought he might even be pro-clingy where Jason was concerned.

Definitely pro that little smile and the way Jason went on tiptoe to brush a kiss over his lips. "You've got my whole dance card filled, Bax."

He liked that. Hell, he liked that quite a bit. Jason's hand came to rest on his hip, solid and hot.

They moved around the little sitting area in front of the bed, long-short-short, long-short-short. He could do this forever.

Mini hummed, breathing in time with the music, trusting in Bax's hold. He loved that Jason never doubted him. Not once.

Nothing had ever made him feel so goddamn big. Ever.

Not even the time he'd won the big Cowboy Rides Away round-robin event, covering six bulls.

Although that had rocked.

Jase sighed softly, his breath brushing against Bax's throat.

"You okay?" he murmured. He just wanted to be sure they were as much on the same page as he thought.

"This is perfect. Perfect."

"It is." *Woo. Thank God.* He took another turn around the room, feeling like a million bucks.

A ride. A dance. A happy Jason. His life wasn't going to get much better than this.

Bax decided to just be right there in the moment as long as he could.

Sometimes that was the best a man could do.

Chapter Nine

By the short go on Sunday, Jason Scott found himself in the amazing and utterly fucked-up position of covering three bulls—one for a ninety-two-eight—and heading for a perfect weekend. All he had to do was ride this last bull, and he was the event winner.

That meant cameras.

That meant an interview.

"You got to throw it, Jase," Dillon said in his ear. "You have to."

Did he? He didn't want to. He wasn't a quitter, and if he won this event? Shit, he was in at the finals. No matter what, he was in.

All event winners got an automatic spot.

He took a deep breath, running his options. Con. He didn't know the bull much. He was fairly new, and Jason had never seen him buck. Pro, the bull was small and went into Jason's riding hand, which was a perfect storm.

"Bax?" He didn't know what he was going to do, but he intended to check in with his touchstone.

"Ride, Mini. We'll figure it out."

"Yeah." That was what he thought. Ride it. Win this event. Get the points and the check.

They could run interference, and he would wear his shades and say he was still sensitive to the lights. Whatever he damn well had to do.

He loaded up, grabbing his bull rope. Dillon was quiet, but Gramps was there, right there in his ear by the gate. "You can do this. You can ride this bastard for ninety. You can."

Gramps believed in him. So did Bax and AJ.

Dillweed didn't understand. Riding was more important than safety. Always had been.

Then again, Dillon was a clown. He'd never known the thrill.

He stopped thinking on it, because this was about letting his body do what it was meant to do. He could do this. Jason took a deep breath in, then let half of it out. His hand was in, the bull was standing up and all he had to do was nod.

Which he did.

They were in the middle, him and the bull, and his world was right and tight. Fuck, this was pure magic, and he loved the way time slowed for the last three seconds. He spurred, his leg moving in time with each leap and spin.

He heard the buzzer, and he let go, landing on his butt for a second before Coke hauled him up and tossed him toward the fence, where he scrambled up, feeling wind on his ass as the bull rushed by. He trusted Coke, and he trusted Dillon, who was whooping, "Run, Jase! Woo!"

He climbed down, laughing hard as he heard the air horns go off. *Yes. Fuck, yeah. Bring. It. On.*

"Ninety-two points, folks!" The announcer shouted, and the crowd went nuts, screaming and clapping.

He waved his hat, and Dillon was there at his shoulder. "You're an asshole."

"Prove it," he shot back.

Dillon whacked him, laughing and speaking into his arena mic, something about what a good first event he'd had back. Then Bax was there, pressing his dark glasses into his hands.

"Thanks. Check, interview and we're gone, right?" He was going to love Bax into a puddle as soon as they were alone.

"You know it. I'll hang out, since your eyes are so sensitive to the light."

He had to grin, because he could almost hear Bax nudging and winking in the words.

"Cool. Good ride, huh? Felt like a dream."

"You were in the middle, Mini. Solid as a rock."

"Good ride!" AJ flanked him on the other side.

"Thanks, man. Felt good. Felt like it ought to."

"Keep that up and the season is yours." AJ lowered his voice. "When they call you out for the check, Bax and I will take you almost all the way, pretending to roughhouse a little. Dillon will bring you back."

"Got it." He felt damn near like he could do it, all on his own.

Not that he would. Lord knew he didn't need to fall on his face *now*.

Talk about awkward.

Funny as fuck, but goddamn bad timing.

He needed to save that for winning the finals. His momma loved that movie where the blind figure skater fell over her roses after she skated like a ninety pointer.

Jason was still grinning when the new interview lady—What the hell was her name? Amy? Anya?—called him over for the check. AJ draped an arm around him and marched him up, Bax blowing an imaginary trumpet or some shit. Good thing they'd always been assholes like this, and he was grateful when AJ deposited him on what had to be his mark.

"Congratulations, Jason. How does it feel to be back?"

Jesus, how do you think? I just won the friggin' event. I'm terribly disappointed. "It's been a long road to recovery, but I'm tickled as all get out."

"I'm sure your fans are excited to see you. Are you planning on going to more events, or just the finals, now that you've won?"

Jason automatically grabbed the big piece of cardboard that whacked him on the vest. The fake check. "Well, I'm here to ride bulls, ma'am."

"Smile, Jason." Dillon's voice was sudden and strong in his ear, and he grinned his best aw-shucks smile.

"Well, congratulations again, and good luck on your next event."

"Thanks!" Jason turned to where the on-camera assistant always was, handing off the big check. His real money would come direct deposit tomorrow.

"Head left, Jase," Dillon said, and he hoped to God the clown meant his left.

Bax grabbed him and fake gut-punched him. "You did good."

"Yeah." He nodded, but he was ready to get out of here now. It was time.

"Come on."

The guys all stepped up to glad-hand him, but Balta and AJ, Bax and Coke kept them all back just far enough by backslapping and laughing until he could change and get the hell out of the building.

Bax let out a gusty sigh the minute they were in their town car. "Whooo."

"No shit, cowboy. Let's go. I want—" Was it fair to say he wanted to jump Bax's bones?

"Yeah?" Bax sounded a little breathless now, and he'd bet Andy got it. He wasn't craving a hamburger.

"Yes. Bad." He felt the truck start up and begin to move, and he reached for his fly.

"Uh, Mini? We're still in the truck. You know that, right?"

"Uh-huh." Jason guessed it was less sexy than he thought, so he stopped touching. No reason to be a dork. Besides, he didn't want to be all hard when he got to the hotel.

"Well, don't stop then!" Bax sounded a little like a foghorn, his voice had gone so deep. The engine revved a little when Bax stepped too hard on the gas, but nothing bad happened, so they must not have been in traffic yet.

"I thought—" He grinned and shook his head. "Damn, man. I thought that was a stop it thing."

"No. No, I was just wanting to make sure you knew there were windows and shit. You're the hottest thing ever…on earth. I wanna see."

"We're up high, and it's dark." He stroked himself through his jeans, feeling friggin' wild as hell.

"Uh-huh. Damn, you smell good, Mini."

"Yeah? You like it. I'm wanting you, Bax. I'm wanting to touch you like I couldn't all them times before."

"I used to just jack off in shower all the time." Bax chuckled, the sound warm as a touch. "I like touching."

"I listened." His cheeks were on fire, but his cock was aching, it was so full.

"Jesus, Jason." Now Bax was scandalized, but he burst out laughing. "Jesus, that's fucked up and hot."

"What was I supposed to do? I wanted you, and…well, you weren't ever going to say so."

"I was afraid you'd stop traveling with me," Bax murmured. "Then where would I be?"

"Never happen. No matter what, Bax. I'm with you."

"That's what I need." They rolled up to what was probably a light, and Bax reached over, pressing a hand to Jason's crotch.

He bucked, rolling into the touch like he was riding. "Bax!"

"Uh-huh. Had to feel that." Bax squeezed some.

"I feel it." He pressed Bax's fingers into him a touch harder.

"Gotta drive, Mini." Bax pulled away, and he moaned.

"Damn it."

"Sorry. We'll be there soon."

"It's okay. I started it." And he wasn't bitching. This was…playing, and it was damn good.

"Oh, hell yeah, you did. Gonna finish it so good." Bax was rarin' to go. That roughness in his voice sent shivers up Jason's spine.

"Fuck, I want you, Andy Baxter. I want to tear it up."

"Yeah, Mini. I want to do it in the shower and in the bed." Now that was ambition.

"Mmm…I like it when we're all wet and slick together."

Bax was panting, he thought. Jason stretched, feeling like a million-dollar champ. That championship was going to come, too. He had no doubt.

He'd get to come first, though. Lord, he cracked himself up.

"What's funny?"

"Just happy, man. So happy."

"So am I, Jase. Seeing you ride like that. Damn." Bax's hand was back, even as they picked up a little speed.

"It felt good." He knew Bax would get it. He had no doubt.

"You looked amazing. Right in the middle, babe."

"Yeah. No pizza party tonight, though. Tonight it's a-a private party."

"Yeah. Room service and a hell of a lot of lube." Bax chortled at his own joke. *Dork.*

"Tell me we can get busy first?" He didn't think he could wait that long.

"Yes. Before we even order. I have peanuts."

Whatever worked. He needed Bax more than he needed to get his feed on. Bax was like freakin' air. He had to have the damn man all the time.

"We're here, Mini. Carry your gear in front so the world doesn't see you springing wood."

"Am I zipped?" He couldn't remember and instead of rummaging around, he lifted his hips for Bax to get an eyeful of his hardness, which he figured was still covered. No air.

"Jason Scott, I swear to God. Come on. I need you."

"Coming." He sang the word, teasing like hell. But he got out of the truck and grabbed said gear bag, as instructed.

Then Bax hustled his ass in, dragging him into the hotel and up the elevator. They made it to the room, both of them flinging shit all over, meeting in the middle for a clench. He yanked at Bax's shirt, tearing it out of the man's jeans.

The buttons on the front of his shirt gave way, and Jason would bet they'd have to send it out the laundry to get them sewn back on.

He didn't give two fresh shits. He needed Bax. Right now.

Bax seemed just as eager, getting them both naked, then dancing him back to the bed. They stretched out, the kiss going nuclear hot. He explored Andy, dragging his fingertips on the warm flesh like he was painting.

Really, he was seeing all that compact, hard muscle, and finding Bax's scars one by one.

He knew where they were, but he felt it was a little bit like playing guitar. Every touch discovered him a new sound.

Bax could be downright loud. The man was amazing. His.

He added his mouth into the game, scraping with his teeth here, dragging his lips there. When he licked at the flat part of Bax's belly, he got a groan that liked to tear Bax in half.

He made sure to nuzzle the wet tip of Bax's cock, nudge it good and hard with his chin.

"Mini." Bax said his name like it was the only word in the world.

"Yeah. Yours." He dipped his chin and sucked in Bax's tip.

"Uhn." Bax stroked his hair, then the back of his neck, which made him shiver, his cock jerking.

He nodded and took more in, one hand cupping the tightest ass in history. Bax was fucking perfect, hard with muscle and stocky where he was lean.

Lord, he was lucky. He had everything he needed, right here, naked with him.

Bax was babbling at him, words falling down around him, and he sucked and licked, wanting more.

He tugged Bax up into his lips, slurping him, dragging his tongue along the shaft.

"Gonna make me come, baby." Bax was panting, and he tasted the pre-cum on his tongue.

Good. He wanted to make Bax *wild*, like he was riding. Bax fucked his mouth, really letting him have it, losing the rhythm a little. He relaxed and let Bax in all the way, pressing into the back of his throat.

"Jason! Jesus!" Bax shot for him, *boom*. Just gave him a flood of wet heat. He swallowed, loving the way Bax whimpered with every gulp.

"Lord have mercy. Come up here, Mini. I want to make you feel good too." Bax tugged at him, demanding access to his body.

He nodded, scrambling up Bax's body, rubbing all the way. His turn was always a damn good thing, and Bax got busy, those rough fingers tracing his skin. "Give me what I need, Bax?"

"Yeah. Anything, baby. Anything you want." Bax gripped his cock, stroking hard.

"You. This. Fuck, I love your hands."

"I love touching you." Bax's voice was breathless and rough, his touch making Jason thrust hard. Jason braced himself with one hand on the headboard, slamming his hips forward. "That's it, Mini. Take what you want. Jesus, you're amazing. I could do this all damn day."

"Yours." The word was the truth, and fuck, he was flying, his balls tightened up like stones.

"I can see your skin, all flushed. You're close, baby. I can feel it too, so wet on my hand." Bax was relentless, not letting up on him for a moment.

He panted, his chest moving like a bellows. Fuck him. Fuck him, this was good. He didn't take much longer before he was flying, his balls emptying.

"So damn good." He could hear licking, and he knew Bax was cleaning his hand, which caused Jason's dick to jerk a little more.

He slumped down against Bax, grinning like a fool. He'd never been so happy. Never.

"I got you, Mini." He had a feeling Bax felt the same way. Fool had always been more invested in Jason's career than his own.

"I'm glad. That felt good, man. That felt real, like I could do this."

Bax pressed a soft kiss to his neck. "Then memorize this moment, Jase. Pull it out when things get tough and remember."

"Yeah. Yeah, I think I will." He wouldn't have a perfect season, but dammit, he had a goal, and he was going to make it or die trying.

"Good deal. Come here and snuggle with me." Bax pulled him down, then tugged a sheet over them.

"I like snuggling." And he loved the blasting air and the heat of his Bax. They made him shiver, and sensation was everything to him these days, making up for his sight.

Andy's stomach growled, making him laugh.

"Moving on to room service, huh?" Bax said.

"Hell yeah. I want a turkey club with bacon and onion rings."

"You got it." Bax rolled them to one side of the bed, and he laughed at the bumpy ride. Then Bax proceeded to order enough food for an army.

"We're just hungry, right? Not having company?" He wasn't wanting to be all social and shit.

"Just enough to keep us a bit. I don't want to have to go out," Bax agreed.

"You're such a homebody these days," Jason teased.

"I got you. I don't have to distract myself no more."

Oh, that deserved a kiss. Damn. He pointed himself in Bax's direction and puckered up, and he got just what he wanted. It was a damn fine day.

Hope was a dangerous drug, but he was high on it.

Chapter Ten

Bax woke up stiff as a board, but in a damn good mood. The last few weeks had been like a dream, Jason riding like the champ he was, the events going smooth as silk. He even liked the hotel, even if they were in North Carolina, where touching and shit had to be cut right off in any public area.

Even careful touching.

Jason was starting to feel the rides, bruises popping up here and there, the sports tape on one knee, the other shoulder. He sure hadn't missed that.

A few people were starting to push too. Ace kept trying to get Jason cornered. It was like watching a very frustrated border collie when they thwarted the damn man.

Which, okay, was possibly more fun than color TV, especially when Dillon and Emmy got in on it. There was a delicate dance with them, where Coke and Balta were more like a polka band with lots of accordion.

Jase had ridden one of two, and it was Sunday again. Time for the short go.

Bax took a deep breath, then reached for Jase, wanting to get a little kiss in before it was time to get up and hit the strategy meeting with the guys.

"Mmm…can't we just skip today?"

"Nope. If you place today, we can take a few events off, huh?" Bax had already talked to Coke about it. He wanted to not go up north for the next two events, where more people had cameras and only a handful of riders really got attention. Those Yankees took Jason's lack of autograph sessions personally.

They needed to go see Momma, they needed to rest—and they needed to plan for the next leg of their life.

"The numbers make it work still?"

"They do. You're chugging along. You get top four and we're golden."

"That's what I want. Ace is pushing. He called twice last night."

"Yeah." Bax shook his head, then laughed when he realized Jase couldn't see. "What are we gonna do about him?"

"Call him from Momma's?"

"Now, there you go. Just tell him you never got the chance to catch up with him." Jason was so much smarter than him.

"That way you, Momma or Jack can holler if I get in trouble."

"We can." Bax rubbed his hands up and down Jason's back. He loved how Jason was taking control, grabbing onto the bull rope and hanging on.

That needed to be a trend. Jason was gonna have a lot to learn after this season.

Still, Andy approved of this new, confident, re-energized Jason. He wanted the man bad, in fact, but if they got busy, they would lose track of time.

And Jason was always hotter after a ride.

He grinned, his body liking that idea a lot.

Jason stretched, sliding against him. "You're happy."

"Yeah. I can wait." He could. They probably needed a shower.

"It can be my reward for riding…or not riding. Either or."

"It can." Every bit of him was Jason's. Period.

"Good deal. You want to go down for breakfast? Go out? Order up?"

"Let's order up." Just to hide a little while longer. They could do that, right? The breakfast places at the host hotel were always like bear traps.

"Excellent. I want pancakes then." Yeah, Mini never ordered messy food in public.

Bax felt so damn honored that Jason would get all sticky with him.

"Two sets of pancakes, two sets of sausage and two coffees?"

"Perfect."

"Cool." Bax called it in, chatting with the lady taking his order, whose name was Lilah, and she was about to get off work after the night shift and go babysit her grandkids.

Jason padded off to the bathroom, and Bax got lost for a second, just trying to figure out when he and Jason had started figuring this shit out—hotels and weird bathrooms and how to deal.

He would probably just sit down and cry, but his Mini counted steps and felt things and had learned so much. Dillon was good for that, always doing research online, making calls. The guy had a damn organized brain for a clown.

And Jase was determined, dammit. He wanted this. Bax wasn't sure what *this* was exactly, but that was okay.

Grinning, he shook his head. He'd always been a bit of a follower. He'd let Jason pick the path, then, by damn, he would do all he could to help make that path clear, even if it took a machete and a flamethrower.

Maybe that was why things were working now. Jason had always been the one in front, and when the accident had happened, he'd been thrust into the position of making the decisions.

Bax listened to the water run, stretching hard. His knee popped when he got up to grab some clothes so he could be dressed when the food came, and he grimaced. Man, he was becoming one of them old has-beens.

"Looking forward to heading to Momma's, Bax? I sure am. I want to start searching for properties online with you."

"I am." The way Jason said that made his heart thunder. Living together. Like permanently. Buying their own damn land. Hoo-yeah.

Jason walked out, naked as a jaybird, then headed toward the window where his jeans and tighty-whities were on the chair.

Bax stared, because well, why wouldn't he? The bruises on Jason's back made him frown, because they were awfully close to the kidneys, but the rest? That was all smiles for Bax. "You ready to ride today?"

"I am. I'm more ready for my time off. I'm tender in the back. Not terrible, just tender." Jase's eyes lit up with laughter. "You know me. I'll leave it in sports medicine."

"I know." Jason would get a bunch of attention from Doc's assistant, who he thought Dillon had let in on the game, and he'd be right as rain in time for the ride.

Jason got dressed and started packing. They'd get on the road tonight, stop a few hours out and get there in the morning.

The knock came at the door, so Bax got the tray and left the tip, then set up breakfast. "Come on. Eat your gooey stuff."

"I'm so in. Tell me when I can deal with the butter. Is it on top?"

"It is. Like a ball. One of those they make with the scoop. Just on the one."

Jason found it with his fingers and slipped it in between, chuckling with mischief. "Ta da!"

"There you go. Syrup is to the top right in a creamer thing. The little metal ones. I moved the actual cream so you won't mix them up." He wanted to lick Jason's fingers.

"Thanks, Bax." Jason dipped his fingers in the syrup, playing with Andy.

He cleared his throat. "You're a mean man, Jason Scott."

"Wanna taste, Andy Baxter?"

"I do. Give me some sweet stuff, Mini." He leaned, knowing Jason knew right where he was.

Jason painted his lips with that sticky finger then brought them together in a playful kiss.

They needed to take this good mood into the ride today. Keep the wave going. Jason rode better when he was confident and relaxed.

He kissed Jason easily, slowly, making sure he got all the syrup. He loved this, how Jason opened up, offered him everything like it was easy. Bax guessed it was. Loving Jason was easy as falling off a bull, so maybe it worked both ways.

"I do like breakfasts like this." Jason leaned back and cut a clumsy bite of pancake, humming as he managed to get it in his mouth.

"Me too, babe. I love pancakes." *I love that you trust me.*

"You and me both, cowboy." Jason got him, heard him—and Bax knew it.

He kissed that mouth one more time before stealing a bite. Good thing he still worked out with Jase.

"They're good, huh? The butter is the best part."

"It is. All melty." Hotel butter was the best. Some things just didn't taste the same at home.

His phone buzzed, and he grabbed it, checking his texts. *Coke. Shit.*

Coming up.

"Dammit."

"What?" Jason was already starting to frown. "Is someone coming up? Tell them we need ten minutes."

"I'll try, but it's Gramps."

Give us a few to get dressed.

No problem. I'll grab coffees.

"He's getting coffee. That will take half an hour."

Thx

"Thank you. I got pancakes, and I want to finish them, dammit."

"I want that too." Gramps was a good guy, but he worried about Mini too damn much. He had all this pent-up guilt.

"Gramps is fucking obsessed." And it sounded like Mini was getting tired of it.

"He means well." Bax leaned over to fork up pancakes and syrup. "Open up, baby."

Those lips parted like a dream, making his belly tight for a second. Then he popped the bite in, and Jason hummed, smiling again.

The mood swings were disappearing Th these days. That meant things in that hard head were improving, he thought.

He kept hoping that Mini would wake up and suddenly see again, but it ain't happened yet.

Most likely wouldn't. He'd been reading and reading online. Braille. Seeing-eye dogs. Canes. Adaptive tech and shit. Jason could have it all soon as he won.

Then they had a whole fucking lifetime to be together.

"Hey, can a guy get another bite?" Jason did the *ahhh* mouth.

"So demanding." Feeding him did go faster.

"That's me. Demanding. Feed me. Love up on me."

"Tell me which way to go at the elevator. Hold my hand." He flicked his fingers against Jason's arm. He couldn't just wink no more, but he liked being physical.

"Tell me which way to go? Drive me all around."

Okay, this was getting less funny.

Bax hoisted up to lean over the table. "Kiss me some more, Mini. That's my favorite." He pressed his lips to Jason's.

There was his smile again, just like the sun coming out. *Good man.*

"You just don't let Gramps get to you." Bax said. "You focus on riding."

"You got it. I'm the cowboy with the plan…uh…boy."

"Nice rhyme." He laughed out loud, and they finished up breakfast just in time for the knock on the door. Bax checked them both to make sure they were presentable before going to let Coke in.

"Hey, y'all. How goes it?" Coke carried four coffees in a carrier. "Dillon's on his way up."

"Cool. Just finished up breakfast."

Coke glanced at Bax, his eyebrows rising. Yeah, so he'd said they were getting dressed. Sue him. Gramps didn't say a word though, which was good. It wasn't none of anyone's what they did.

The second knock came not much later, and Bax let Dillon in. The guy always had five times the energy of everyone else in the room.

"Hey, guys. We ready for a good show? This is the probably the last show Emmy's going to have with us. That baby's getting close."

Jason chuckled softly. "At least Cotton's here with her."

"Yeah, knowing that kid's luck, the pyrotechnics will startle the baby right out of her tonight," Bax said.

"That would keep Ace off my ass, huh?" Jason sounded tickled to death.

"It would. How you gonna do that long term?" Gramps asked.

Jason shrugged. "Call him from Momma's, like I told Bax. I cain't stand there with him. He'll know. He's the smartest cowboy on earth, after Balta."

Andy nodded. That was true, and Jase's eyes moved like wild things, if he were honest. Ace thought it was damn rude to wear sunglasses when someone was talking to him too. "Smart or not, Ace'll reckon Mini if he sees him."

"Yeah." Dillon sighed. "Okay, so you call him from home. We'll figure it out."

"Yeah. Bax figured out what all I need to do to win the championship. I can do it."

Andy watched Coke blink. "You think so, son?"

"I got to, Gramps. I got to. I want to announce my retirement and go have my life."

Coke's face crumpled a little, but Bax knew he was proud. It showed in those gray eyes, shining bright. "Well, then, you got to share the math with me, Andy. So I can help."

Dillon did a little dance step. "Ditto. I have an accountant brain. I can make a chart."

Jason relaxed back against the headboard. "We're gonna buy a house on the beach, and I want a dog."

Dillon coughed, choking on his coffee until Coke slapped him on the back. "Sorry. Like a guide dog or a ranch dog?"

"A guide dog. I mean, ranch dogs too, but mainly a guide dog. I need to learn shit, and we'll figure it, but we got us a plan, me and Bax."

"Well, okay. That works for y'all." Coke looked… Andy wasn't sure. Was that bittersweet? It was less than tickled and more than sad. "Make sure you have a guest room. I like the beach."

"Yeah. He likes to bake his bones. So are you gonna win, place or show today?" Dillon asked, changing the subject, which was probably fine.

"I've already showed, so I'm reckoning on a win. I want to earn my vacation."

"Well, then we need to make a plan for the interviews. You did okay last time, but they're gonna want you to do that five questions BS soon." Dillon chewed his lower lip, thinking hard.

"I can't, Dillon. I cain't stick my eyes straight, man. They'll think I'm stoned or something." Jason sounded damn near panicked.

"Well, unlike with Ace, you can wear your sunglasses. Just tell them the light hurts your eyes still. Schmaltz 'em."

"And y'all can't tell with the lights on me?"

"Not with the glasses on."

Bax nodded. Dillon had the sharpest eyes, so if he said no, then that was that.

"Hell, you get too worried about it, just limp off the dirt like you're a little hurt and they can tell everyone you had to go to sports medicine. Then we hustle you out." Coke was the man with a plan.

"Right. I'll wing it." Ah, the Jason Scott motto. *'When in doubt, wing it.'*

That hadn't changed one bit. Andy was okay with that. Made life interesting. Unless Jason was trying to drive, which had happened.

Coke checked his phone. "I swear, the weekends just get shorter and shorter. We're heading to Dillon's place after the event to spend a couple of days."

"Good deal." Bax glanced at Dillon, who was smiling at Coke, but there was an edge of worry in his eyes. *What is that about? Gramps had better not be hurtin' again.*

Personally, Bax thought Gramps ought to retire and start having some fun. Seriously, all the man did anymore was cowboy protection. They went to Dillon's, but that was like physical therapy, so Gramps could soak in that huge hot tub Dillon had put in.

They needed to go to Mexico or something. Go deep-sea fishing. Take a cruise. Disappear for a few months. Something.

"Huh?" He blinked. He'd missed something.

"I said, are you all geared up for today, son?" Coke was frowning at him.

"Sorry." Bax chuckled. "Thinking about Momma's chicken fried steak."

"Oh…" That was a great sound that Jase made. Pure goofy male happiness.

"Damn. Don't make Coke want to go south instead of north," Dillon complained.

"You'll make me pot roast," Coke murmured. "And carrot cake."

Dillon shimmied again. "That I will."

Gross. Dillon still freaked him out a little bit.

Coke hooted, and Jason shook his head. "I can tell I'm missing a visual."

"Bax has 'ew' face on," Dillon said. "He just went there thinking about me and Coke."

"Did not. You're just not natural."

"Oh, he's all real, boyo." Coke sounded satisfied as hell.

Bax gagged, clutching his throat and really working it.

Laughing like a loon, Dillon jumped on him, giving him a noogie.

"Jase! The clown is molesting me!"

"Make sure you wash the makeup off before you kiss me, then."

Jason's words made him stop and blink. Their friends knew him and Mini were…well, together, but this was new. This was just saying it, right out there.

It felt… damn fine. Even better to struggle away from Dillweed and go swing Jason up out of his chair and around the room.

Mini kept his eyes open the whole time, just like he was riding a bull. Sweet.

"Okay, y'all. Drink up." Coke was getting his business voice on. "We need to talk bulls. I got the short list. If you can, take Mama's Boy. He'll make you look good and he's on fire."

"He is." Mini's expression went mulish. Jason had him read the bull stats to him every week before the event. He knew all there was to know.

"Good deal. You know who you drew for today?"

"Knocker. He's kind of a booger, but if I can stay out of the well, I can do it." Jason's lips curved. "I got good balance still, at least."

"Nate and I will do our best to keep him from turning into your hand," Coke said.

"Y'all rock. It'll be what it is." And now Jason wasn't going to talk about it anymore. Bax knew that expression.

Coke and Dillon both looked at Bax, and he just shrugged. He wasn't gonna try to force his man to do nothin'.

"Guys, easy. It's bull ridin'. That part I understand. It's the part after the bull that's a bitch."

"Sure. We're just cabbage heads." Dillon whacked Coke's arm. "Come on. Let's go for a drive to the arena. Take a few minutes to ourselves."

"I didn't mean to run y'all off…" Jason looked like he wasn't sure if he was relieved or worried.

"You didn't." Coke snorted. "Dillon's just telling me we need to stop mother henning. We'll be there when you ride, son. Don't you worry."

"I don't, Gramps. You'll always be there, telling me where to run."

Coke's eyes shimmered a little. "From your lips to God's ears, son."

Dillon rolled his eyes dramatically, but Bax knew better. He was having the feels too. They hustled out, and Bax chuckled.

"Alone again."

"Isn't that a song?" Mini laughed for him…or at him. It was hard to tell.

"I think so? You know that shit better than me." He rubbed the back of his neck. "You want to listen to anything? Or just hang out?" The time before they left for the arena was always just tense.

"You want to get out of here too? We could drive around."

"Hell, yeah." Bax set the alarm on his phone to half an hour before they would have to be parking at the event. "Let's do it, babe."

"Sounds like a plan." Mini reached down and hunted for his boots, stomping right into them. "Let's do this. I want to go home and see Momma."

"Me too." He wanted to breathe. Bax grabbed their go bags, as eager to get this over with as he used to be to ride.

Lord, he was getting old.

Chapter Eleven

Heavens, it was good to be home, but weird? Christ.

"Jason! Andy! Y'all made it!" Momma was already crying. "Jack made brisket. and I have all the stuff to make chicken fried steak. How's the wrist?"

"Still broke." Jason'd cracked it but good on his short go ride, but he'd taken the event and used the injury to keep from having to glad-hand. He reckoned that worked out.

"Well, come in and I'll get you some ice and a pillow to rest it on."

"Just the pillow, Momma," Bax said, muscling in bags behind him.

Jason could tell from the grunting.

"You want some help, Bax?" He had one good hand.

"I got it. Hey, y'all. Ice will just make the little cast wet, Momma."

"Ah. Well, here's that pillow." She pressed Jason to a chair. "Want a Coke?"

"Sure. How are y'all? It's good to be here."

"Good, son. Good." A chair scraped back, Momma's knees brushing his as she sat and put his wrist on the pillow. Jack must be at the fridge. "You're riding good. I-I couldn't hardly believe it."

"No, me either, but it needs to happen." Jason knew as soon as the suits got wind of this, he would be toast.

"You looked good, son," Jack said, setting the Coke down with just enough of a thump that he'd know where it was. "You need to work on your left side a little. You're leaning."

"Am I? That shoulder's getting tired fast. I'll keep my mind on it. Thanks." At this point, he was taking advice from everyone. He guessed that was the good Lord's way of teaching him humility or some such shit.

Bax snorted as if he'd said that out loud, so he ought to watch his tone.

Momma was just fluttering, patting his leg and making Momma noises.

"I'm okay, Momma. I'm good. Me and Bax are great." He grabbed her fingers and held them. "It's okay. I missed you."

"Jesus, I'm glad you're home. I needed to see you."

"I'm glad to be here." He was. Jason had no idea what he'd do without her, but her worry made him itch a bit. He hated making her feel bad.

"I am too." Bax landed beside him. "We need a couple of weeks of downtime, and we're fixin' to look at property down on the coast."

"You are?" Momma sounded utterly gobsmacked.

"Yes, ma'am." Start out like he could hold out.

"Yeah. Be a nice compromise between being close and having something of our own." Man, Bax was just toughing it out. Jason was damn proud.

"And I want to live on the ocean."

"What about hurricanes?" Momma asked. "And sharks?"

"Brenda!" Jack just cracked up.

"Well, I can still board up a window, Momma. And you get tornadoes." He couldn't hold back his grin.

"And unless it's a giant mechashark," Bax drawled, "I can handle it."

"Wouldn't that be a megamechashark?" he asked, barely holding in his laughter.

Jack snorted, then hooted like a big owl, and his momma slapped his leg.

"Making fun of me. You just have to let me get used to the idea. This is new."

"Not that new, but yes, ma'am. I reckon you two will be coming to visit a lot."

"I like the beach," Jack said mildly. "Saltwater cowboys. Sounds good."

Bax laughed now too. "It does."

"You just want to go fishing. Still…I like the shrimp down there, and it's not a bad drive."

Oh Lord, please don't let Jack and Momma buy the house next door.

"Just get something with a good guest suite," Momma said primly. *Oh, whew. Good deal.*

"We'll make sure," Bax agreed.

"You're good boys. I'm going to see if it's supposed to rain today." Getting rid of Jack was easy.

"Mmm." Jason made that noncommittal noise all ranch people made about the weather and eased his fingers over the table to find his Coke.

"You want anything to eat, son?" Momma asked. "Andy?"

"Don't get up," Bax said. "We can nibble until it's time to have… What time is it, for heaven's sake?"

"Damn near three. Y'all made good time."

"We left last night, spent the night in a motel." And fucked like bunnies on the squeaky mattress. That had been fun.

"Lord. Did you check for bedbugs?"

"Yes, ma'am. Clean as a whistle." Bax touched his shoulder. "Crackers and cheese, Mini."

"Thank you." Oh, there was something about the smell of cheese. Nothing else smelled like that, even though lots of things smelled like it. It was also easy to eat. Finger food. Even in front of his mom, who had seen him rolling in his own poop when he was a baby, Jason was self-conscious.

That was one of the first things—learning from folks as soon as he could. He didn't want to have to hide no more.

There were even schools, and a cowboy had his pride, but Jason wouldn't spit in nobody's eye if they could teach him not to be worthless as tits on a boar hog.

He had to be Bax's partner in all this, not a layabout.

They chatted with Momma and noshed, but soon enough he was nodding a little, all the travel and his broken wrist catching up with him.

"Hey. Momma slipped out with orders to go take a nap," Bax said, hand back on his shoulder. "Wanna?"

"Uh-huh." He headed back without thinking. Between Bax's hand and the years he'd stumbled from the kitchen back to bed, he never even hesitated.

"Bed's already turned down." Bax sat him down and tugged off his boots a few moments later.

"I'm all babyheaded, man." And that was no lie.

"Been a long couple of days." Bax crawled into bed with him after a little shuffling. "You did it, though."

"We did. Thank you. I can't imagine doing it without you."

Bax kissed his chin. "I wouldn't do it for anyone but you, Mini. I love you fierce."

"I know." Jason never doubted it. Not for a second.

"Mmm." Bax wrapped around him. "You think we're selfish, wanting to go to the beach?"

"No. We want to do it, so we should." Bull riding had asked a lot of him.

"Okay. I just wanted to make sure. Momma looked shocked." Bax's breath stirred the tiny hairs on his neck.

"She doesn't think that I would ever leave, not now."

"She don't know you like I do…as an adult." Bax had a point. He'd always be a kid to Momma. That was the way of it.

"I think that's natural, huh? Mommas are that way." Hell, they saw it with Missy all the time.

"Yeah. Yeah, you know me. I missed out on a lot of that."

Bax just didn't have good people.

"You have her now, though. Before we were us, even." Momma loved Bax, had taken him under her wing like he was hers.

"I do. And Jack is a good guy." Bax kissed him again, then cracked a huge yawn.

"Uh-huh. Sleep." He curled into Bax, finding where they fit. "Rest for a while."

"Okay, Mini. I can do that." Bax went boneless just a few minutes later, a soft snore sounding.

It was good to be home for a minute, somewhere they could rest and let Momma do all the worrying.

Chapter Twelve

"Hey, Mini! That real estate lady wrote us back," Bax called to Jason, who was sitting on the porch in a plastic kiddie pool, his feet up on a footstool Jack had made out of a wooden cable spool.

"Yeah? She find anything good?" Jason looked tan and happy, about as rednecky as he could be.

Bax opened the email on his tablet, scrolling through. His footstool was way more hairy…and drooly. Jack had a new dog, a bloodhound and Great Pyrenees mix. The silly mutt was named Emmit, and he loved Bax already.

Bax kinda liked him too.

"Two good possibles. Listen to this. This one has a guest house with a bitty kitchen and a hot tub."

"Oh, that's cool. Close to the water?"

"Yeah. It's not right on the beach, but there's a path. Kinda across the street." Bax hummed. "The other place is right on the water."

"Yeah? What's it like?" Jason looked like the happiest cowboy on earth, and Bax snapped a picture to send to Aje and Gramps. They'd both get a kick out of this.

"It's a little smaller. Has a mother-in-law suite instead of a guest house. Has a good little plot of land, though. Enough for some horses. No hot tub, but that we could put in. It's a little more out of town."

"Cool. I like out of town and on the water. And we need room for a couple horses and some dogs."

"I think so, yeah. It needs more improvements, but it ain't like we ain't got the money." He tapped out a quick email with his hunt and peck typing, telling Monica the real estate lady that one was a real possibility. Maybe they could go have a tour.

"Cool. Maybe we could go see it." That was his Jase, following his brainwaves. "Well, you can see it, I'll feel of it—and together we'll figure it."

"Sounds good. I wrote the agent." Excitement curled in his belly. Whether Jason won or crashed and burned, they could do this, and it would be a sound investment.

It wasn't fancy, and it would take work, but he liked to do that sort of thing, and God knew they had friends who did too.

Coke was a machine, and AJ loved to build shit.

He grinned, happy as all get out at the very thought.

"If there's enough room to let someone stay the night, a place for a TV and a comfy couch and a bedroom for a—" Jason stopped and blinked, his expression dumbfounded.

"A bedroom for what, babe?" He held his breath, not sure what would make Jason look like that.

"We'll get to buy us a bed, Bax. Like you and me. Together. One we pick."

"We will. We'll need something firm for my damn back." *Look at that smile.* It lit up his whole world. He got it, though. They had places and beds and shit all over the damn country, but wasn't none of it theirs.

This would be the first thing that was.

"We'll go to one of them mattress places and lay on every damn bed in the store," Jason teased, splashing his hands in the water.

"Lord yes. We could get one of them magic number beds."

"Bah. I don't think we ought to get a bed that can break, Bax." Listen to that wicked man.

"I reckon not." No one else was there to hear but the dog, and he wasn't gonna tell. "We'll give it a workout."

"That's it. Do you like a big headboard deal? One with drawers?"

"I can go there." He didn't care, really, but he would bet that could be handy to hide supplies in—and keep shit away from said dogs. Lord knew, Coke and Dillon's bassets was always digging out weird nonsense from people's houses.

"Cool. I like that idea too. Drawers are always good for stashing stuff." Jason chuckled softly. "So, couches? Recliners?"

"I like a big couch. One of them that has recliners on either end but a big middle. So we can sit together. Room for dogs and all of AJ's kids."

Jason snorted. "That would take three couches."

Hell, it might take five. "It's Gramps and the clown that'll be around the most."

"Mmm." Jason nodded. "We'll get the guest bed with them in mind. One of them adjustable ones where the head and feet go up and down."

"Yeah. Yeah, Dillon would love that for Gramps." Jason was a good guy. A real good guy, no matter what they said about him down at the jail.

"Cool. You think I could learn to read braille?"

"Whut?" That took him a minute to transition. "Sure. You're a smart dog."

"I was hearing they make labels for food and shit in braille, so I could find the peanut butter."

"Yeah. And if it's our place, we'll put shit where it goes, like in the little fridge in the trailer." They had a system. It wasn't fancy, but it worked.

"I'm a lot of work." Jason looked smaller all of a sudden.

Bax scowled. "No, sir. No more than me and my bad knees and worse temper. You stop it."

He wasn't having that shit. Jason Scott had made more money this year than he had in five. Jason's name was what was going to keep them afloat, not his.

And Jason was his North Star. That was that.

Mini grinned, stretching, looking like that happy man again. "Well, okay."

So there. Bax rubbed that dog with his toes. This was the good life.

His phone beeped, the real estate agent answering him. "That house is still available. You want to run down day after tomorrow?"

"Yes, sir. I surely do."

"I'll tell her." He might see if he could put in some kind of earnest money too, Bax had a feeling about the place. It had all the things they needed—space, beach, land.

Their place.

Bax took a deep breath, filling his lungs with new air, letting out the old. Sometimes a man just had to do that.

Let himself believe a little, that this—all of this—was going to be real.

Bax got up, scaring the hound half to death, and scooted his chair across the porch to where he could dangle his feet in the kiddie pool. "Oh, that's good."

"Right? We filled it with a couple-three bags of ice."

"Smart man." Bax sighed, leaning back and closing his eyes as he tugged his hat back.

This he could get used to.

Chapter Thirteen

The plan was to get in the truck, run down to Corpus, look at the place—so to speak—spend the night in a hotel, and run back to Momma's.

Bax was in a great mood, and so, by extension, was Jason, both of them excited to maybe do this.

The radio was on, they had the windows down and Bax was singing, which was pretty nice, actually. Jason felt freer than he had in ages.

Bax was excited. Jason could hear it in his voice, in the songs and the random chatter and the frequent laughter. He knew Bax had put down some money to keep them in the race for this place, but he hoped there wouldn't be any long, drawn-out bidding war.

If they liked it, they'd just buy it.

Cash tended to speak.

"You said this place had stairs?"

"Yeah, it's on stilts for hurricanes and all. That worry you?"

"Nah, we'll figure it." Hurricanes and storms were part of living near the coast, just like tornadoes came with East Texas and sandstorms and floods came with West and Central Texas. "This whole state will try to kill you somehow, huh?"

Bax hooted. "True enough. Just trading one thing for another."

He just wanted to be able to hear the water when he was sleeping. The waves would soothe his soul, he knew it, and he wasn't that much of a philosophical man.

"Maybe we ought to get a little place in the mountains, too," Bax mused, sounding almost drunk with the possibilities.

"Yeah? We could do that, something little to enjoy in the summertime." They might have to save for that, given that he wasn't sure what all he was going to do for money once the riding was done…

"Yeah. I mean, we'd need to do improvements on the main house and all first, but I still got those sponsorships, and that home improvement place wants me to do some commercials." Bax took a deep breath. "They're offering five hundred thousand for three, Mini. They say I got credibility."

"Go for it, man. Dillon says there'll be a book deal, a movie deal, lots of interviews and all, once the shit hits the fan—and that will bring money too."

"Cool. I just need to make sure they can schedule it when you're not at the show." Bax touched his leg, which was bouncing and he hadn't even known it until then. "You nervous or excited?"

"Excited, more than anything." He felt a little like he was at a precipice, standing there at the edge of a whole new thing, and he intended to jump, dammit.

"Me too. Hopefully it doesn't smell like beans or old farts."

Jason hooted, Bax's words making his chest tightness ease.

"We'll just spray Febreze." God knew they carried it everywhere, just in case. "So it's two stories, on stilts, balconies all facing the water."

"Yeah. Mother-in-law's suite, master up with the bathrooms. Downstairs there's two little bedrooms and a kitchen-front room deal. A big one."

"That'll be great when everyone comes. We'll need us one of them outdoor kitchens like Coke put in. Everyone from Gramps to Balta and Beau and Sam will want to cook for us." Jason knew they needed that and a hot tub. They could do some bubbling, him and Bax.

Poor Bax had that damn arthritis in his knees, and God knew what all else Jason was gonna break before this was all over. Like they all said… It wasn't *if* you got hurt. It was *when*.

"We're heading in. I can see the ocean. Can you smell it?"

Jason rolled down the window, inhaling deep. He could. *Goddamn.* "Yeah. Yeah, Bax. I so can."

"That's pretty cool. It's a pretty day." Bax was gearing right up. That voice all but vibrated.

"I can tell. The wind's blowing, the sun's out—and we're here." Together.

That was a little too silly to say out loud, but he meant it.

Bax patted his leg, then went back to singing, and he didn't exactly count the minutes, but he figured it was another thirty or so before Bax turned on the GPS, muttering about weird goat path roads.

"You love an old dirt road." *Isn't that a song?*

"I do, but not when I'm trying to find a place for the first time," Bax bitched.

"No stress. Are we late?"

"Nah. We'll be fifteen minutes early, if'n I can find it on the first try."

"You'll do it." Bax was the king of finding hotels and arenas and weird-assed things in the middle of nowhere. It was a skill.

Thank goodness, or he'd never go anywhere.

Jason snorted. This was the age of Uber. He was fine.

Shit, he was more than fine. He had managed to fool the world into thinking he was just a grumpy shit. Which, okay, he always had been. *Thank God for that now, huh?* He'd never been one to do the autograph events.

"You're bouncing again, Mini. It's gonna be okay."

"Not scared. Excited." Energy just buzzed through him. He knew they weren't going to find the perfect house on the first try, but they were getting to do their damndest.

"Ah. Hold on." Bax turned suddenly, and one arm came out across Jason's chest. "Sorry. This should be the road it's on. At the end. Nice. Not much else out here."

"Oh, good deal." That was one of the things he and Bax both needed. They weren't city folks.

Hell, they weren't even suburban folks.

"I wonder if more of the land would be available—just a few more acres." They slowed, turned again and Bax parked. "Looks like she's here, so maybe we can just go on in."

"Okay. I— How do we do this, Bax? Without her finding out about my eyes?" He was suddenly scared of jumping.

"Get your sunglasses on. I'll give you all the visual clues, and we tell her you're sensitive to light due to a head injury. She's a Texan, so God knows she should understand bull riding." Bax sounded so certain, so he took a deep breath and nodded.

"Right. I hadn't even worried about it, and…" Pure, stupid panic. He grabbed his glasses and put them on. "Let's go find us a home, Andy Baxter."

Chapter Fourteen

"So, let me know if y'all need me, and I'll just let you wander."

Bax smiled and nodded at the real estate lady, glad she was fixing to leave them alone. Jason was tense next to him, jaw set, because she'd just gone on and on about all the features of the house, and they were still standing in the big front room.

It was big and empty, all tile and wood everywhere. The kitchen was decent-sized enough, with one of them island deals to sit at, along with room for a kitchen table, which was good.

"Where do you want to start, Mini?" he asked.

"Show me what's what?"

"Well, this is the front room." He glanced at Monica, who had stepped outside to the decking and was on her phone. "It's got just a few pieces of stuff in it right now. What do they call it? Staged? But you could have a dance in here." Hell, their voices echoed.

"Is it nice?"

"Normal, not fancy like a hotel lobby. It looks like a house, somewhere you could live." Bax liked it. It was a place where there'd been water and sand and wind. "The whole damn downstairs has this wraparound decking with these huge windows and screens and fans. That's nice as hell."

"Oh, that's cool. We'll use that."

"Hell, yeah." He took Jason by the arm. "Kitchen is open concept at the end of this room. There's a big island then a U-shape." He led Jason down there, let him feel his way around, starting at a huge pantry cupboard, then the stove, a big double sink, counter space and ending on the other side with the fridge.

"Oh, this is nice. Easy to figure out." Jason explored the island. "So, can you see outside from everywhere?"

"Yeah. Even the lower level. The floor down there is stone. Up here it's wood, and the deck is that composite stuff. Looks redone. There's some stuff to do, but the appliances are stainless." He watched Jason feel the countertops and the cabinet doors.

"Rock on. So the little bedrooms are down here, and then the two masters are up?"

Good memory. "That's right."

He led Jason down the hall. "There's a powder room by the kitchen and a laundry, but the big bathroom is to your left."

"Cool. Is it decent?"

"Yeah. The bathroom will need an overhaul. I want a walk-in shower for it, but there's room." They kept on, the two smaller bedrooms just so-so. They headed upstairs, finding a great sitting room loft deal. This was cozy as fuck, somewhere to sit if he couldn't sleep. The first master was...plain. That was okay. They could make it theirs. "This is huge. Not much to it, but it's a nice blank canvas."

"That's all we need. That and a big bathroom."

This bath had been redone, with a walk-in shower, a big old Jacuzzi tub, everything. "This is nice."

"Shit, you do echo in there. Shower?" Jason asked, and he whistled.

"Big one. And a fancy tub. I can bubble."

"That's good for your knees." Jason reached out, just touching anything within his grasp.

"Nice and clean. Let's check out the mother-in-law suite, huh?"

Jason grinned. "Our official company space."

"That's it." Bax took Jason down the long hall to the addition, which he had to admit, they'd worked in seamlessly. "Wow. This is nice, babe. There's even an apartment-size stove and fridge and sink."

"Shit, really? We'll never get the folks out. AJ might move in."

"Missy would kill him." Bax looked around. "It's all set up with two twins, but there's room for a queen, and we'd put in a fold-out sofa for the kids."

"Yeah, and we could put something like that in one of the rooms downstairs too." Jase looked happy. "Can we go outside up here too?"

"Yeah, although up here is just open to the weather. There's balconies." He headed outside to examine them, finding them solid. He'd want to triple-check each slat, because if Jason miscalculated and fell, shit, that might kill him. There were some single-level houses in Corpus, but nothing like this, with water access and room for the animals they wanted to keep.

"Come on out." He reached back through the slider, taking Jason's outstretched hand.

He led Mini out, noticing how Jase turned right toward the sun, face up, like he was soaking in the light. He could smell the ocean, the salt and humidity hitting him, and he could just imagine the maintenance it would take to keep tractors and trucks running and not rusted.

Good. He needed to keep busy. So did Jason—at first he'd have schooling, then? Who knew?

The only guarantee was that Jase would blow the doors wide open, no matter what he chose to do. His man was a brilliant fuck.

"You're squeezing my hand. What's got you all worked up?"

"I really like it, Jase. We could be comfy here. The land will need a little work. There's some good fencing, but we'll need to level out the horse areas with some good fill dirt to keep them from getting hoof problems."

"We could do that. We got time after October. Spend the winter fixing things up, then get some livestock." Jase bumped shoulders with him. "You want it?"

"I do." Bax would need an inspection report to know what all really needed to be done, but he wanted it. They had the money to sink into repairs, especially if he did those commercials.

"Then let's do it. The beach is close? We can get in the water?"

"We can walk to a couple of inlets, babe. Or we have a stretch of beach that would probably be better to four wheel to, but you can get back and forth even on your own if need be. It's just a hike." He'd read up on why these houses out here by the coastal islands couldn't be right on the beach, but if Jason had a dog? Yeah. Bax would rather go with, but he knew his stubborn lover.

They'd come up with a system. Hell, he could run a rope fence all the way down to the water.

"That works. I just want to be close enough to get in the water."

"Me too. There's a garage, but it's a ways away from the house. I bet we work that as a shed for tractors and build a carport for the truck." He was getting starry-eyed. They needed to talk turkey to Monica first.

"We'll figure it all out, right? Let's go make an offer." That was his Mini. Pull off the Band-Aid. Just do it.

"You got it." They headed back in, hand in hand, and he got Jason set up at a stool at the kitchen island. "Let me get her."

"Hey." Jason's voice stopped him in his tracks. "I love you."

"I love you too, babe." He did. So much.

God knew they could do an awful lot with that.

Chapter Fifteen

"We did it, Momma."

"What?"

"We put an offer in on a house." Jason listened to Bax in the shower, his lover singing like a grasshoppery bullmoose. "I'll send you a picture in a bit."

"Son, how many houses did you see today?"

"This one." This was the one they wanted. "We found the right one first."

"Well..." She paused, and he knew 'Momma voice' was coming. "Are you sure you shouldn't look at a few more? Just so you're not disappointed?"

"I'm sure. It's perfect, Momma. Perfect and right. You're going to love it." He proceeded to tell her all about it—the mother-in-law's suite with its own kitchen, the sunroom that wrapped around the whole house—and the ocean, right there.

"That sounds real nice. I could make my own coffee," she teased. "I'll get Jack when we're done, and we'll look at the link."

"Good deal. I'll know more tomorrow." They'd made a cash offer at considerably lower than asking price. They knew they wouldn't get it. They just wanted to start out low and give themselves some wiggle room.

"Well, good luck, baby boy. I'm proud of y'all. Both of you."

"Yeah? Thanks, Momma." He wanted her to be. He wanted her to know how hard and scary all this shit was.

"Do you need anything?"

"No, ma'am. We got us a hotel and room service and we'll walk on the beach in a bit. We'll be back up with y'all tomorrow."

"Okay, I love you. Send that link, now."

"I will."

Bax would, but whatever. Someone would teach him better how to do that.

There had to be a voice thingy, right? Some way to tell his phone or the laptop to send links and shit.

He'd bet there was. Still, right now, he'd wait on Bax. Speaking of… "You fall asleep in there, man?"

"Huh?" The door opened in a cloud of Old Spice-scented steam. "I was feeling gritty, huh? You want it next?"

"I do. I called home. Momma wants a link to go look." He stood and started stripping down, making sure to put today's clothes in a separate pile from tonight's.

"Cool. I'll send it. Man, that shoulder is all bruised up still." Bax came to drop a kiss on his bruises.

"Is it? It don't bother me nothing like the itch in this stupid-assed cast." He hated them, but Doc always put the hard ones on him, saying he'd just wreck the soft ones.

"Let me bag you up. You need help washing?" Bax sounded a wee bit guilty.

"You can sit and talk to me, if'n you want." He wasn't going to have to do much. Momma had buzzed his hair for him yesterday.

"Cool. Let me hit send." Bax tapped at the laptop, then came back to him to help him get undressed and to wrap his arm.

"So, when do we get to start being excited? Soon?" The house was empty, so they'd asked for closing in fourteen days, leasing for the time in between. That way they would have a house before they headed to the next event.

"Shit, babe, I already am. Monica seemed pretty happy, and they've been using the place as an Airbnb. Unsuccessfully, apparently. Why the hell wouldn't they take an offer?" Bax got the shower going again for him.

"Right? I'm tickled, and I can't wait to sleep there. Once we know, we buy a bed first, right?" He stepped into the tub, letting Bax balance him on the slick.

"We do. We'll get it delivered and set up and all, get sheets at the same time. They'll be more expensive there, but they'll also make us a deal." Bax got him steady, the steam feeling like it was melting the salt on his skin.

"Oh, this is good. You gonna have to paint the walls?" It occurred to him, all of a sudden, that he didn't know what color the walls were, and he never would. Never again. He'd never know colors again. He didn't know what his house looked like. He didn't know what it looked like from the windows.

His knees tried to buckle, but he kept them firm. No. No, he was not fucking ruining this with that sort of bullshit. This was a good thing. He was going to fucking be grateful and thank God that they could buy a house, him and Bax. Together.

"You okay, Mini?" Bax couldn't see him, but his lover always knew, didn't he?

"I was having a mo. I'm fine."

"Well, God forbid you have them mos," Bax teased. "The walls are pretty good. We might need to go from fake wood to tile in some high traffic areas. Them boards is warping."

"Works for me. I like tile. It stays cool."

"Yeah. There's a lot of sand out there. Like a lot, a lot. I think we should put in an outside shower, to keep you from going crazy crunching sand under your feet."

He laughed out loud. "You saying I'm picky?"

"I'm saying you can't sweep as well as you used to could."

"Good point. We'll get one of them Roomba things that does carpet and tile." That was a compromise, right?

"Oh, I'll put that on the list." Bax had a list? *Rock on.*

"Yeah. I figure we—well, it's on my phone, but I've started a list of some things I thought of. I figure we'll hit up the Walmart for some pots and pans and dishes, just to get us started." Man, Bax had been putting thought into this.

"Towels. Peanut butter. Forks and spatulas."

"Bread to go with the peanut butter. I figure your momma can help with that list too." Bax cackled. "Look at us, setting up house."

"Lord, I bet Momma comes with a truckload. She set up the travel trailer, didn't she?" She was good to him.

"She did. That woman has more shit in her storage room than I've ever owned in my whole life." Bax's chuckle was warm and fond. Yeah, he was family.

He soaped up his short hair, just using the Ivory soap bar. "Was there a security system deal?"

They weren't going to be home all the time.

"There was one of them doorbell cameras, and one at the gate, but nothing in the house." Bax hmmed. "I'll add that, too. Expensive man," Bax teased.

"Yeah, but we ain't home for a while sometimes." Gramps had folks to watch his place when he was gone.

"True. And we ain't gonna have anyone real close." Bax paused. "You know I was just teasin', right?"

"Well, shit yeah. We got this. I'm nervous, though. I want to know it's ours." He didn't want it up in the air and all. He was ready to put down roots.

"The waiting sucks." When he turned the water off, Bax was right there to help him dry off. That broken wrist was shit for anything but, well…anything.

"You know what you want to eat tonight?" Jason asked, turning in the towel. "You want to order room service then go walk?"

"Sure. I'm down. Unless you want to get finger food at some shop. Then we all look like fools and make a mess."

"Maybe as a snack." He would rather have something at the room, and the hotel was nice enough.

"Cool. I'll read you the menu."

"I want cow and potatoes." He was going to learn how to eat a steak, dammit, without someone having to cut it up for him.

"Well, they just happen to have a sirloin or a ribeye."

"Sirloin." That way he didn't have to do the minefield of fat. There was no good thing about crunching down on a boingy bit of gristle.

"Baked potato? Salad?"

"Baked. Do they have coleslaw?"

"They do." The phone clacked as Bax picked it up and punched up room service. Lord, the hotels they stayed in these days were a far cry from the roadside motels they'd stayed in at the start of their careers.

And they were fixin' to buy themselves a goddamn beach house. Wild.

He grinned, just feeling good in his bones. Even the broken ones. Jason knew he had to focus on the now, get the riding done. But he was so ready to be on to the next stage of life.

Was that fucking weird or what? Was this just being grown up? Or was this being in love and making a home?

Maybe it was both. There was no going back now. Him and Bax, they were an 'us'.

"Dinner is on order, babe." Bax sat next to him, kissing just below his ear, which made him shiver. "There's smoke coming out of your ears. Whatcha pondering?"

"I just—" It felt silly to say it out loud. "I'm ready for this, and I never thought I would be—and that's weird."

"Yeah." Bax took his hand, playing with his fingers. "You know, we think we're invincible. Then we find out we ain't. It's tough."

"Yeah. I— You stuck around. You didn't have to, and you did." And Jason wasn't sure what he'd done to deserve it.

"We're a team. I pull your rope and always have." Bax leaned on him. "Is it weird that I got a burger and a salad and carrot cake?"

"You and your cream cheese icing." Nah, it wasn't weird. It was Bax, so it was okay.

"Yeah. I need it. Doesn't mean I won't get ice cream later." Bax maintained that ice cream was a thing at the beach, just like corn dogs were at the fair.

"I like that. Ice cream, I mean." He chuckled softly. "It's going to take a little while to figure out all the different stairs in the new house."

"I know. I figure we'll get us a system. Something on the railings where you know which set goes where." Bax was always thinking. Dillon had taught him a lot about that in the last year or so, to think outside the box.

"Maybe a couple baby gates for the beginning. We'll need them for dogs, too, right?"

"We will. They'll need training." Bax leaned on him, just humming a tuneless little ditty.

"Yeah. Yeah. I hope they take the offer." Excitement and nerves warred with each other, making him a little queasy.

"Me too. Let's distract ourselves." Bax kissed him then—nothing hard or urgent, just, "let's make out until the food comes."

Normal shit.

Easy shit.

Everyday—

Bax's phone rang.

It clattered to the floor. "Shit!" Bax scrambled. "Hello? Sure. Is it okay if I put you on speaker?"

"...just wanted to let you know that I have an answer from the sellers."

They both held their breath, which whooshed out of Bax when he had to answer. Jason tried not to laugh hysterically at Bax's voice breaking.

"Okay?"

"They accepted. We can sign the papers as soon as you'd like."

"Holy—" Bax cut himself off. "We can sign tomorrow if we can get one more walk-through in the morning. And we'll need to go to the bank."

Bax would want to look at the plumbing and electrical, he'd bet.

"I'll meet you in the morning. Say nine a.m.?" And just like that, they had a house.

"Sounds great. Thank you, ma'am." Bax's phone clicked off, and they sat there for a long moment.

Then Bax whooped, pulling him to his feet and dancing him around the room.

He couldn't believe it. He just couldn't. They'd bought a house.

"Lord, Jase. Our house. *Ours*. Let's get a bed before we leave town."

"Okay. Yes. Tomorrow. God, Bax. Tomorrow." He was floating…just fucking floating.

"I know!" Bax kissed his mouth hard. "I'm so proud I'm about to bust. You should call Momma."

"Yeah. Yeah, You ought to call Aje. We'll tell Gramps and Dillweed together." He grabbed his phone and told it to call Momma.

"Hello? What's wrong? Are y'all okay?" Lord, mommas would always be mommas.

"They accepted the offer. We got it, Momma." *Please be happy for me. I need that like anything, 'cause I'm trying so hard not to be a tittybaby. Please have my back.*

"Jason! Congratulations, baby. I can't believe you found the one you wanted so fast, but you always know what you want. Well, I just can't wait to see it."

Oh. Yeah, she was tickled.

"There's room for guests, the water is right there, we'll be able to have horses… It's a good place, Momma." He couldn't stop grinning. "I told you there's a suite with its own little kitchenette and sitting room and everything, right?"

"You did! You're never going to get the cowboys out of there. You'll have to make a calendar."

"You know it. And it's an easy drive for you and Jack." He loved the idea of her coming to see him. He would feel less like a little kid going home.

"Shit, son, you just tell me when and we'll bring a trailer's worth of goodies! Me and Jack had tons of extras and we've just been holding them in storage."

"Oh, Momma. Thank you." He could hear Bax jabbering to AJ, and he had to smile. It meant everything to him that Momma was gonna get on this bandwagon. "We start the process tomorrow, then we're gonna go buy a few things."

"When do you close?"

"The lady says a week to ten days, but we'll just lease until the paperwork is done, so we'll be in sooner."

"You want us to come over the weekend? We can bring y'all some stuff, help you get things put up and celebrate your new place?"

"That would rock. Then we wouldn't have to drive back up yet." Jason jittered his leg, thinking hard. Bax would want to get in there and look at electrical and plumbing. Jason wanted to get a grill, maybe a couch.

"Good deal. It'll give y'all a couple days in your house alone too. Y'all need that." She sniffled softly. "I'm so excited, baby."

"So am I." This way they could make sure the place was clean enough for Momma, too. She would get the white glove out when no one was looking. She worried so. "Y'all bring bathing suits and beach shoes."

"We will. Fishing poles? Is there a deck?"

"There is. A wood one. Nothing fancy." Nothing about the house was fancy, and that worked for him. He didn't need that. They were boys with sand and fish guts and cow shit.

"Oh, that's fine. We'll bring you a bunch of old towels and all for the deck, and fishing poles we got a ton of. Jack loves to ocean fish."

"Well, y'all come on. We'll have lots to do, and we'll figure it." Hell, Momma might have fun.

"We will. We'll see you Saturday midmorning."

He'd bet they would be up before the sun and there by nine. "Yes, ma'am."

"See you then, son." They hung up just as Bax was saying, "Okay, Aje. Cool. Thanks, man. Bye."

They sat together and breathed before Bax asked, "You ready for me to call Gramps?"

"Let me just grin a minute."

"Was Momma good?"

"Yeah." Yeah, he thought she genuinely was. She was worried about him, but she was happy. She trusted him, which was a huge thing. "She's coming this weekend and bringing us a trailer of shit."

"Well, then we'll just get some furniture and some basics and see what all she brings." Bax sat next to him again. "No sense buying anything she can give us."

"Right? We'll find us a bedroom and a couch and a big-assed TV." There was so much to do—utilities and shit, Internet. All of it. Starting tomorrow.

"All right, babe. I'm calling the bullfighter and the clown." Bax's phone engaged on speaker, and it rang once. "Hello?"

"Everything okay, son?" Gramps sounded tired.

"Put us on speakerphone, Gramps!" he called out, hoping this would perk his oldest friend up.

"Sure." There was a clatter, a "Shit," then a crackle that meant they were live. "Shoot."

Bax grabbed his hand. "We bought a house!"

"You *what*?"

Dillon was right there. "When? How? What the hell?"

"We did." Jason couldn't stop grinning. "Just out of Corpus. Got enough land for some horses. A few outbuildings. Water is right there."

"No shit?" Gramps sounded utterly shocked, then he started to hoot. "Really? Tell! Tell!"

So they did it again—telling about the sunroom and the dock, the guest suite and the balconies.

Dillon laughed right out loud at that. "You'll have to make sure you don't go over, Jase."

"I'm going to take care of it. I was hoping Gramps would help me add another set of rails to the upper balcony, and we're going to run a rope down to the dock." Bax had this planned out, didn't he?

"Sounds like a plan," Dillon said. "There's all sorts of things we can do to the outbuildings, too. Maybe gravel on one walkway and something else on another."

Jason loved how Dillon thought of them as family now. 'They' did shit, not 'y'all'.

"We'll come down for the week before you ride again, fair? I'm taking a few days off here." Damn, Gramps was pooped.

"That's more than fair, Gramps." He smiled toward Bax. "More than."

"Hell, Momma and Jack are invading this weekend, and Jack will want to help," Bax agreed. "Don't you worry on it."

"We'll be there. We may fly in then ride with y'all. We'll figure it." Dillon wasn't worried. "Send pictures!"

"We're heading back over in the morning for the walk-through, so I'll take good ones," Bax said.

"Good. Congratulations, kids! I can't wait to see it."

"I'll send you a bed for the guest suite as a housewarming, guys. Just send me an address tomorrow." Dillon didn't sound like he was going to entertain an argument at all.

"You're the million-dollar clown, man," Jason agreed. Coke needed the best, damn it.

"I am. Tomorrow. Address. Go celebrate, boys."

Like it was meant, a knock came to the door.

"That's our food," Bax said, rising. "Later, Gramps."

"Bye, y'all." He hung up and sat there, listening to Bax bring in the table.

They'd bought a house.

The food smelled amazing, and his belly rumbled. "Thanks, Bax."

"Anytime." Bax walked him through his plate, but didn't momma him, letting him do his thing.

"We bought a house. Does it feel fucking weird to you?"

"Hell, yes. Tickles me to death how surprised everyone is too, like we don't know how to do shit."

"Well, we are fuckups of the highest order, man."

"We are. I mean, did you know you was blind?" Bax hooted, slapping the table hard enough to make it creak.

"I am?" He slapped himself on the forehead, then they both cracked up.

The steak was so perfect, and Jason knew he had to savor it. Days like this were few and far between.

Most days were hamburger, and some he just had to drink his milkshake through a straw.

Not today. Today was sirloin, all the way.

Bax made the happiest noise, and he knew Bax was right there with him. And there would be ice cream for dessert.

That was a damn fine thing.

Chapter Sixteen

Bax took a deep breath, standing at the door to their house, keys in hand. A couple three days ago, they'd signed everything. Now they had lights and water and more in their name, no realtor in sight and the bed, a fridge and a huge sectional couch were on their way in two hours.

"You ready, babe?"

"I think so. Open the door." Jason was standing at the top of the stairs, vibrating.

"Okay." He did, the brand-new key sticking a tiny bit, but it worked. It was just the humidity and salt. Bax was already making lists of things that would take a different kind of maintenance than a small ranch in East Texas.

"We're in. Come on, Mini. Take that step."

Jason stood there a second, then nodded like he was riding, and came right to him and they stepped through the door.

He took Jason's hand and tucked it in against his arm. "You ready to count off the kitchen while there's nothing in the way?" The staging furniture was all gone. They had a blank slate.

"Yeah. We're at the front door." Jason stepped forward and they counted. This was easy. They'd done it in a hundred hotel rooms, at Gramps', AJ's. Jason was quick, absorbing all the information.

He just had to make sure he matched his steps to Jason's natural ones. The first few times, he'd waltzed Jason about, and Mini had run into things. 'Easy does it' was better. Jason trusted him to get it right.

"Okay, so reach out now and you have the kitchen island at arm's length."

"Are we going to put chairs here? To sit at?" Jason walked around the island, searching it with his hands. "Are there counters all around us?"

"To your left, there's a pantry cabinet that's pretty big, then a little counter, then the stove as you start around the U. The sink is in the middle, directly across from the inside of the island." He watched Jason feel his way. "Then you get more counter and cabinets, and the fridge will be at the other end of the U, where you come back past the island."

"Cool. I like it. It feels good—not crappy, not fancy."

No, it was right in between. Just perfect for them. "There's a nuker above the stove and the dishwasher's…yeah, right there."

"Oh, cool. I can do that without having to move too much. Not like Momma's where they stuck it in next to the fridge on the same water line as the ice maker."

"Right?" Bax took a second to look around, letting himself take it all in. His house. This was somewhere he belonged, something he owned, something permanent and real. He was damn proud, and Jason couldn't stop grinning, which made it even better.

He could see them, a year or two from now—all their shit around them, dogs and more animals to care for, sitting and listening to the water.

Bax sucked in a breath and held it a second, fighting a rush of shit that he didn't know how to feel. He sure wouldn't be able to explain it to anybody.

Jason came around to him, hunting him with outstretched hands, then hugging him close. Lord, it was like Mini felt vibrations from him or something.

Still, he'd take it. He held on tight, breathing with his man. "We got us a house, Mini."

"Yessir, we did." Jason sounded about as wigged as he felt.

"There's not even a place to sit. We should have got us some camp stools."

"We can sit on the floor. God knows we do it enough at work." Jason chuckled. "After the couch and all comes, we'll run to the Walmart and get some food and outside chairs and sunscreen."

"Sounds like a plan." That way they could figure out where everything was from their place, see how long it took to run errands. Bax liked a plan.

"We need a big TV with speakers too. And something to play music everywhere. Baby gates. Whoa."

"I'll start a list." They just sat right on the floor where they were, and Bax pulled out his phone to make notes.

"We'll have to bring the fifth wheel down too and park it here. That'll be nice, to have room for it." Jason chuckled softly. "You going to decorate with antlers and horseshoes, man?"

"Hell, we'll be lucky if there's anything on the walls two years from now."

Mini snorted. "Dillon and Emmy will provide art if we don't. Keep that in mind."

"Oh God."

"Right? Momma will help. Then you'll have sunflowers and horseshoes and a lot of wood signs and shit." That would be better than a bunch of naked dudes cavorting and tons of heavy glass vases on posts.

"I need the AJ decorating school," Bax said. "Comfy couches, warm blankets and a few good Western paintings."

"Amen. I mean, it ain't like I'll notice."

"You will if it's itchy or smelly." He leaned on Jason, thinking how tonight they would sit on their couch and watch a movie, then go to their bed.

"We have to buy a comforter and some pillows." Jason grinned. "A soft one."

Thank God the washer and dryer had come with the house. They would have a lot of towels, too. Momma had said she was bringing old ones for the beach. "I'll shore up the parking situation soon, and Jack can help me put in an outdoor shower."

"Good deal. So…can folks see us on our balcony?"

"Nope. We got no neighbors for half a mile. So unless there's a boat out there…"

"So, if we had a sturdy lounge chair, we could—" Jason blushed dark.

"We could and now we surely will. That might take a trip to Lowe's. I'm not sure Walmart makes fucking chairs." Maybe they did. They'd have to look.

"You'll have to test them out," Jase teased, beginning to cackle at him. "Jump up and down on them some, maybe. Or ask Beau and Sam for recommendations…"

"I like that. I'll call." He would, too. "Though I reckon Balta would be the one to know, huh?" It was a blessing to have friends he could tease.

"Balta's as big by himself as both of us put together! All he'd have to do is flop down. Boom!"

"See? He'll know what to buy," he said, laughing like a loon.

"Did we call him?"

Bax shook his head, then rolled his eyes at himself. "Nah. I texted him. He's been busy, so I just wanted to let him know without any pressure."

"I texted Beau and them too. The Taggarts are close enough to just visit on a whim."

"There are Taggarts everywhere." Adam and Bryan and Chrissie got around. Bax loved them so hard.

"You know it." Jason chuckled. "We need a grill, man. You burn good meat."

Bax added a pork loin, seasonings and a grill to the Walmart list. Their bank accounts were smaller, but life itself was just fine.

Hell, after he did them commercials… They could do this. They had this.

"Let's go walk to the bathroom down here, and I want to explore the sunroom."

"You got it." They both climbed to their feet, wandering all over the main level, then checked out the downstairs, too—and the garage, which was the closest outbuilding.

"Monica said they used to park a food truck in here. That's why it's raised too, to keep water damage out."

"Cool. Is it big enough for the fifth wheel?"

"It might just be." Then they wouldn't have to worry on it. They had room to anchor a carport on a slab near the house that would survive most anything, and

Corpus wasn't as prone to the big storms as, say, Galveston. Bax would do some measuring before they brought down the big trailer. "Looks solid as a rock."

"If it doesn't, we'll figure something else. Hell, you could have a workshop." A moment of sadness crossed Jason's face, then it disappeared. "We need a practice barrel out here, for fun."

"That's a good idea, Mini." They would find Jason's new thing. Maybe they'd set up a little music area in the sunroom. Jason loved to play the guitar. "I'll ask AJ how he set his up."

"Sounds like a plan. Does it feel real yet?" Jason's grin told him that this wasn't a question coming from worry, but from joy.

"It feels fucking amazing, babe. We got us a place. Just ours. You feeling all adult yet?" Bax felt like a big faker sometimes, but today he felt real. Proud.

"I am." Jason lifted his face to the sun again, looking like he was this sun worshipper cowboy type. "I can smell the water, Bax."

"I know. You good?" Hell, he could see Jason was, but he wanted to hear it. Bax needed to know Mini was in a good spot. It was a hard road they were riding.

"I am. I'm going to ride my ass off. I'm going to take the championship. I'm going to come back here, to our house, and get me learning and a dog."

His man with a plan.

Bax just grabbed Jason and held on like he did when he was riding. He was nothing if not stubborn. "I'm with you."

"Then we got it." Jason bumped shoulders with him. "I think, for now, we'll need a set of ropes out to here and out to the water. I can get to the truck just fine."

"Yeah. I can do that." He'd been thinking about how to anchor things so the wind and salt and all wouldn't be too much of a factor. Bax loved that he was going to flex his working man muscles and get some shit done.

He was going to make them a home, make this place right for them. *Dammit.*

So. They would go hit the Walmart once the big furniture came. Grab some food. Then he would make sure he had enough daylight to string some of the ropes Jason would need first while he let Jason set up some of the fridge and stuff like he wanted it. Mini did great as long as things stayed in the same place every time.

They were going to sleep in their bed in their house tonight. Jesus. That brought goosebumps all up over his skin.

They just sort of sat there holding hands until they heard the big delivery truck pull up. Then they grinned at each other again.

"Time to get to work, Mini."

"Yessir. I'm on it." Jason chuckled softly, then they both started howling, letting that hint of sorrow out. A man had to laugh sometimes, so he could re-right his shit.

They did have a hell of a lot to do, though, so the moment had to pass. They got up and got moving, and Bax wouldn't let Jason fall.

Not even for a minute.

Chapter Seventeen

Jason woke up, fighting the panic when he couldn't remember which hotel he was in. He had to pee, so he reached for the wall. If he followed it, he would find a bathroom. All hotels worked that way. Bed. Bedside table. Wall.

Oh. Okay. Window. Open window. Door?

He reached for the door handle, curious, and almost immediately, Bax covered his hand.

"No, Mini. I haven't checked that balcony yet. You hunting the bathroom?"

"Oh. We're at the house."

Bax chuckled. "Yes. First night. Every sound is waking my happy ass up."

Bax led him to the bathroom. "Double sink, then the toilet."

"Thanks." *Christ. Wild. Seriously.*

"Yeah. No problem." He heard Bax humming, probably wandering around, waiting for him.

He did his business, more awake now and less freaked. He explored a little bit, then headed back to bed. Momma would be bringing his TV for the bedroom and the noise would make it easier.

For Bax too, he would bet. That was how they drowned the noise at hotels, so they were both used to the TV.

When he came out, Bax made sure he was back in bed before taking his turn, then came back to slip under the sheets and cuddle with him.

"You'll get used to it soon, Mini. Me and Jack will shore up the balcony this weekend, just to be careful."

"Thanks. I… I don't want to be useless." He didn't want to believe that he'd never see this house.

"You're not. You're gonna work with Momma to set up the kitchen and front room so you can get around. Be firm with her."

Yeah, Momma would try to put things where she thought they went, but Jason had ideas.

"Right. It don't take me long to reckon things. You know that." He'd learned more in the last set of months than he'd thought he could. "I got a knack for this getting-around thing. Hell, I even went to the Walmart today."

That was scarier than getting on the back of a damn bull.

"I know." Bax rested their foreheads together. "That was something. Man, we can spend some money, huh?"

They'd gone a little wild. A grill. A little kiddie pool like the one at Momma and Jack's to lounge in. Sheets and towels and food and TP and all the basics to set them up for a week or two.

"Yeah, but it's a good thing to spend on. I feel like… I feel like this time it's not throwaway. This is real." It was stupid, but he didn't know how else to say it.

"I hear you." Bax was stroking his back, just random touches with no real rhythm. "I love the grill. Wait until we fire it up and test what it can do."

"Hamburgers. Beer-can chicken." Hell, they'd bought the smoker attachment for brisket.

They'd wait until Coke and Dillon came for that. Momma would be kinda insulted if they tried to outsmoke her and Jack. Maybe they'd do a turkey for her.

Bax chuckled. "Mmm. Borracho chicken. Yessir."

"Hell, hot dogs are best on the grill, right? And we got us some good steaks." Steaks and baked potatoes were the bomb.

"We even got that good salt." He could hear the pride in Bax's voice, and he liked to think it was for him. He was eating steak. That was like a huge hill on the learning curve.

It was crazy, the shit he'd never thought was going to be hard. Then again, some stuff was easier than he'd ever expected.

Staying on a bull. It was the 'get off' that was deadly.

"Smoke's coming out of your ears, Mini." Bax squeezed him tight. "You ready to get up? It's still dark outside."

"No. No, just…can we play some music on the phones? I'm not used to these sounds." And he was tired. Really, genuinely tired.

"Good idea." Bax rolled away from him, and soon enough, the Midland radio thing he liked so much on the streaming service was playing.

Then he was held in Bax's arms, and it was okay. He had a place in the world, and it was right here. Bax was solid when everything made him dizzy, and that was good enough for Jason.

He rested his head on Bax's chest, listening to Bax's heartbeat, to the steady breathing as Bax dozed off again.

He could do this. He could. *Please God, let me be okay.*

Chapter Eighteen

Bax straightened up the quilt on the back of the couch, making sure it looked nice.

Jason didn't care, but Coke and Dillon would be there in twenty, and Dillon was, like, a decorating guru or something. He liked shit to look decent.

"You got the ice chest all set up, Mini?" he called. He'd set Jason to getting the cooler filled with ice and Cokes and beer—and getting cups and all set out on the deck.

Lord knew they had everything they could ever need or want, save for the dogs, after Momma and Jack had come through like a whirlwind. Even Dillon's special-order adjustable bed was in the guest suite.

Momma had brought not one, but two trailers full of shit. Kitchen stuff—from a toaster oven to cast iron to pot holders and ten thousand kitchen towels. An iron, ironing board, dressers and end tables, everything from Jason's old room, tools and shit from the barn at the house, a huge roll-top desk that she'd been saving, a map case that had come down from Jason's Daddy's family and six—count 'em—*six* rocking chairs for the front porch.

She'd had a ball.

He and Jack had fetched and carried for two days, and Momma had helped Jason set up the porches so he could get around, making sure everything had a place. They hadn't even fought about it.

"I got it," Jason hollered back. "We got any snacks?"

"Shit yes." Not that Dillon and Gramps wouldn't come loaded for bear. They were damn near as bad as Momma. "We got sausage balls warmed up, them roll-up deals and good nachos."

Jase only wanted queso when it was just them together, so they could laugh about the drips.

"Finger food." He heard Jason fumble at the door for a second, and he wanted to go help so bad, but he knew it wouldn't be welcomed. Jason needed to learn it himself, and he was doing great with the system of ropes. The balcony and the porch were shored up, and there were sturdy gates at the tops of all the stairs, just in case.

"Hey, Gramps, y'all found us!"

"We did. Lord have mercy, son. This place is like a beach palace." Coke's heavy boot treads rang on the floors and Bax went to join them.

"Hey, Coke. Dillon."

"Hey, Andy, Great bones on this place! And the view! You did good." Dillon winked at him and handed him a six-pack. "We brought brisket and all the fixin's."

"Awesome. We got the smoker, so it's a win-win." He went to tuck the beer away while everyone gave hugs, then came back to oof as Gramps pulled him into a big one, pounding his back.

"I like it. A lot. I brought fishing poles. Y'all got licenses?"

"Got them at the Walmart this week." He wasn't sure how much Mini would fish, but it couldn't hurt.

"Good deal. We'll drop a line." Coke looked tickled, but under the smiles, he had bags under his eyes. Bax figured he shouldn't ask now and embarrass the man, but he would corner Dillon later to ask how the man was feeling. "You want the tour?"

"Just show me where to drop the bags and where the Cokes are."

"You got it."

"Jason can show me the bathroom," Dillon said, making a wry face. "I didn't want Coke to have to stop at a fast-food place."

Jason tilted his head. "Y'all didn't bring the dogs?"

"My sister is watching them this time," Dillon said. "They're traveled out for a bit."

"Oh, bummer. I was going to get them floaties." He grabbed Dillon's suitcase and led Coke up the stairs to see the suite with its little kitchenette and sitting area with Momma's old comfy love seat in it.

"Look at this!" Coke seemed tickled shitless. "Oh, this is perfect."

"You like it?" He was about to bust with pride. "We got your bed all put in and everything. I got to tell you, Jack says he's gonna get one for him and Momma."

"Right? They're amazing. Oh, y'all did good. Look at this balcony!" Coke went right out into the sunshine. He was going to have to make a bet with Jase on how long it would take for the clown to buy big, fancy chairs for out here.

Probably not even a full day. Bax was all over it. Coke deserved some comfort.

"Neat, huh? They're all around the whole house. We're just in love with the place."

Coke grinned back at him. "I bet you see a lot of us."

"That's one of the reasons we chose this one. There's a place for folks. There's more bedrooms downstairs."

"Are there? How hurricane-proof is it?"

Bax shook his head. "We've seen all the flood reports on the place. They did the best they could to make it solid as a rock."

"Good deal. I like that there's a fridge up here. Ice and cold Cokes."

"Yeah, and you could make eggs or whatever on the little stove and not have to navigate the stairs." Bax thought this was one of the greatest things about this house. Room for folks.

Him.

Wanting visitors.

Who'd have thought it?

"Well, and you two would understand that. This is real fine, son. Real fine." Coke came back in, looking a little younger.

"Thanks. And you need to take a little nap, you just say." He grinned at Coke. "Seriously, man, this is a no-stress zone."

"I appreciate it. I might do that in a bit. First I want to have a drink and a sit."

"Well, come on then." He led the way back to the main part of the house. "Cokes in the fridge, and in the cooler out on the deck."

"Oh, the deck. I bet Jason and Dillon are out there already."

They did find them out there, laughing and easy together, like friends.

"What's funny?" he asked.

"We were talking about inviting Beau and Sam out after the season's over, going deep-sea fishing and the six of us goofing off for a couple weeks." Jason grinned at him, and he found himself responding to that smile, all the way.

Bax moved to Jason's side like they were attached by one of their ropes and Jason was pulling. "I'd like that. I bet they would too."

"You look as happy as a dog with two tails, Andy Baxter." Coke plopped down in a rocker with a grin. "Damn, y'all. This is a good place."

"It is, huh? You need a pillow, Gramps?" He knew Coke liked one for his neck.

"I got it." Dillon handed Coke one of them travel pillows, and he popped it around behind his head. Now that was a fine thing. He wondered if they made ones like that to go around a bum knee.

He bet they did. Folks made all sorts of shit nowadays.

"So are you going to run cattle on the land?" Coke asked. "Is it real marshy?"

"It needs some clean fill dirt for horses, so I bet we might run a few head for the taxes, but that's it. We talked some about goats."

Dillon clapped his hands. "I love goats."

"Of course you do," Jason said, laughing. "You're a clown."

Dillon drummed on the arm of his rocker. "Bingo."

"I'm going to get dogs." Jason had that determined face that Bax was seeing, more and more often. "And I'm going to figure all this out."

"Sure you are, son." Gramps nodded like Jase could see him. "I have no doubts."

"Thanks." Jason relaxed a little. "I keep thinking that I ain't gonna be worthless as a bag of wet mice. I'm gonna earn my keep somehow."

"Well, we're going to get you a movie deal, man, and a book deal." Dillon always sounded so sure. "Once this is done, you watch and see."

"Yeah. Well, that will be all fine and shit, but I have to be good to help around here. And maybe do signings at rodeos and stuff. Ace might never let me come back to the show to do them, but the smaller venues will."

Bax was so damn proud of Jason for not giving up.

"The sponsors dictate who comes, Jase, just remember that." Dillon chuckled, and the clown's expression was pure evil. "You don't stress that. Once the finals are over, you'll have this in the bag. I'll help."

"So will I," Coke said. "You know that."

"I do. Y'all are good friends—y'all, Beau and Sam, AJ and Missy. Even Emmy and Cotton. That girl have the baby yet?"

"No!" Dillon's eyes went wide. "She's the size of a tank."

Coke snorted. "And you know, Cotton is tiny. My bet is she's having twins."

"I can't imagine." Bax wasn't the baby type. Jason was great with kids, and he loved Aje's brood, but…

"Not looking to adopt a posse, Andy?" Dillon teased, and he flipped the bastard off.

Jason, though, he snorted. "No. If we want to visit kids, we have AJ's place. He's always looking for help, and we can get our fill."

"And Emmy and Cotton will have more," Bax said, relieved. "Among others. They'll all start to settle down sooner or later." Just like him and Jase, he reckoned.

Sam and Beau. Even Balta was spending more time at home.

"That's how it works." Jason surprised him with the words. "It ain't like we got these huge, long careers. I mean, the bullfighters do better than the riders, and the clown? Well, I guess you can work forever, but this is a kids' game. I had another three years in me? Maybe? And that was if I didn't get all hurt in some other way. Let the young guys do it. I want to be someone else now."

Bax found himself nodding, and Coke actually kinda looked…maybe relieved. "Yessir. It's not if you get hurt."

"It's when," they all finished.

Dillon popped open a Coke. "I'll work out my contract. Then we'll see."

"You think you'll do something else?" he asked, and Dillon snorted.

"I think I'll retire with my bullfighter and make a lot of YouTube videos."

Wow. Dillon retiring seemed like this super serious thing. "Who you think will replace you?" Bax asked.

Dillon shrugged. "Lance Jamesby is good. So is Wacey Green."

"None of them are you." Coke looked thunderous, a little, and it made Bax grin. Those two loved each other like…well, like he loved Jase.

"I know." Dillon snapped both fingers, then rolled his shoulders, which Jase missed, but he had to know Dillon was being a goof. "But they'll bring in their own fans, and mine will learn to like whoever takes over."

Jason chuckled softly. "It's weird, huh? Cool, but weird, knowing that it's going to be over, but it'll never be over."

"There's always a new young gun," Coke agreed.

"Someone without a bum knee," Bax threw in.

"Someone who can see," Jason deadpanned.

"Well, that got depressing," Dillon said. "What else are you planning besides goats?"

"Hours and hours of home repair," he said, with a wild grin. "I'm looking forward to fixing all the little things, making this our place, you know?"

"It's a good feeling," Coke agreed. "Dillon and I turned both our houses inside out to make them work for each other."

Dillon hooted. "Hey, I just put in a hot tub. And an outdoor kitchen. And a media room…"

"And I put in a music system in and out, and a doggie door, and added double seats in the media room," Coke shot back. "Thank God y'all only have one house to redo."

"We're talking about getting us a little cabin too," Jason said. "Just something small in the mountains."

"Diversify, I say. You need help with that, just holler, since that's more my neck of the woods." Dillon chuckled. "I love real estate."

"Freak," Bax said fondly.

"Totally. But we have this wild, wonderful network of places. The more the merrier."

"I want somewhere we can go see snow," Jason said, which surprised him. Jason was skinny enough that the cold got into him.

"Well, you can come to mine anytime." Dillon reached over to poke Jason gently. "But a cabin someplace like Colorado would be a great investment, and a neat place to go…when you get your book deal."

"Right. After the movie deal, huh?" Jason snorted. "We'll see. First, we got to get me through the season."

"I got a commercial to make too. Well, three of them." Bax's cheeks heated, but he wanted Dillon to look at the contract, make sure he was doing the right thing.

"Well, Andy Baxter. Look at you." Coke slapped his chair again.

"I know. I'm a star." He flexed a little, making light.

"That's it. He's my sparkling star." Jason grinned toward him.

"You guys are goofs." Dillon kicked back, putting his feet up on one of the little stools Momma had insisted on getting them. "Man, this is the life."

"No shit on that." Gramps rocked like he was the happiest man alive. "We'll help do whatever you need, guys. Maybe after a bit of a rest."

"You look worn, Coke. I ain't trying to be mean."

Jason nodded slowly. "I can hear it when you talk."

"Been a hard season, guys. I ain't getting younger. I got one more season in me, but that's it. I'm wore."

Dillon didn't look any happier at Coke's words than he did. "I have two more years on my contract. I can fly out on the weekends, work and come home, Coke. You know that."

"You work, I oughta work."

"Stubborn bullfighter."

Jason snorted. "They come any other way?"

"Nope." Coke smiled a little. "I'm just so tickled for y'all, though."

Bax nodded. They were too. They'd done something that, even two years ago, had seemed impossible. They'd become like a family.

Sometimes he felt a little guilty for how happy he was when Jason had lost so much. He'd do a lot to give Jason his sight back, but he wasn't sure now that he could give this up, this life they were making.

He intended on spending the rest of his life keeping Mini happy. That would make up for any failing he had now and again, Bax figured.

"Who wants snacks?" Dillon asked, not able to sit still for shit. "I'll bring out some plates."

"Do you need help?" Coke asked, eyes still closed.

"Sit, Coke. He's got it." Bax grinned as Coke didn't even bother to argue. Lord have mercy, that son of a bitch was…tired.

Bone deep.

Was that where Mini'd been heading? Him? Shit, he didn't like to think about that, because Mini wasn't done. Almost, but not yet. *Shit. Shit.*

"Smells like it's coming up a cloud, y'all." Jason's eyes were on the ocean, damn near like he could see it.

"It does. We'll set up inside and watch a movie," Bax said. Coke just needed to hang out, and he could put his feet up too. He'd been moving shit nonstop for days.

"This whole sun room-porch thing is great though." Dillon danced inside. "We can get the breeze and not get soaked. I like it."

"Yeah." Jason got up when Bax tapped his shoulder. "The couch is puffy. It has recliners on each end, Coke."

"Y'all rock." Coke stood and they all started carrying in a plate or two. "I think you need a Coke machine out here. You could put beer in it."

"We could put all sorts of stuff in it," Bax said. "Dillon, can you keep an eye out?"

"I am the king of eBay and Craigslist." Dillon saluted. "I'm on it."

Mini managed to get to the kitchen, nibble then find his chair. The sight made him nod. *Better.* Jason was beginning to seem like he belonged here. They'd done well setting the place up, and thankfully, he didn't have to remind Coke and Dillon not to move shit.

Now, they'd have to do a few dry runs before AJ could bring all his kids.

"Are you ready to ride again?" Coke asked, and Jason nodded.

"I know what I got to do, Gramps. I'm going to slam this into the ground."

"You are. That wrist doing better?"

"It is what it is." Jason shrugged.

Hell, Jason adapted so well to injuries that Bax tended to forget he had them.

"We need to find us a PCP down here, huh?" Bax made a note on their kitchen scribble pad. "I'll call Doc."

"Yeah, and an eye specialist. Things change in the medical field every day." Dillon was the eternal optimist.

"Probably have to drive for that," Bax agreed. "But a good doc can call in X-rays and such on the wrist."

Coke grinned. "Be good to have, as much as you trip over shit, Andy."

"Right?" He laughed, but there was a weird look on Jason's face. A distant sort of thing. He didn't love it.

He wanted to ask, but not in front of the guys, so he just moved to sit next to Jason taking his hand, and Jason held on.

"Our place, huh," Jase murmured under his breath.

"Ours, babe."

"Can I get the honors of starting the movie?" Dillon asked.

"Sure, man. Just pick something good. We got streaming and all the DVDs Momma brought."

Jason nodded and found the remote, tossing it right to Dillon like the clown was a target. Damn, that was cool.

Dillon gave him one of those weird, meaningful looks. Bax never could figure out what they meant, so he just nodded. Sometimes he waggled his eyebrows. By now he was thinking what to feed them all for supper.

Maybe he'd just do burgers. Jase loved that, and he could play with his grill…

Jason squeezed his hand, so he made himself relax. If he was that tense, Mini could feel it, then Coke and Dill would see it.

The television came on, and he let himself get lost in the movie, the company—and the fact that he was home.

Chapter Nineteen

"You ready to ride this bitch, Jason?" AJ sounded stressed as all get out. "He's gonna take one big leap out then spin into your hand. He's a mean bastard, and he throws his head up a lot, so keep your back straight."

Bax was holding his vest as the bull shifted and moved beneath him. The tension in Bax's hand vibrated through him. He needed this ride. He needed every ride he could get, but this one had the possibility to make a ninety pointer.

An event win.

He took a deep breath. Then another one. The clock was ticking and he needed to get out of the chute.

"Is he still crouching?"

"He's waiting to jump."

"Fine."

He didn't have a choice, so he nodded, and the gate opened with a clang. Aje had been right—the bastard damn near went vertical out of the gate, and he bore down, telling himself not to let his body slam forward into the bull's head.

That would suck.

His wrist ached, but Jason gritted his teeth, ignoring it. He sat up and counted seconds in his head. Three. Four. Kick. Spur.

"Riding you," he bit out, forcing himself to keep his eyes wide open. "Fucking riding you."

His free arm stayed up, his chest stayed out, his hips moving—and the buzzer sounded, just about the time his feet blew out the back.

"To your right, Jason!" Dillon screamed in his ear, and he threw himself that way, that big horn grazing his cheek. *Jesus.*

Jason felt the bull rope wrap around his cast and pull, hard. Suddenly he was flying, dragged in circles, and the best he could do was to keep his feet on the ground, his head in the crook of his arm. "Coke! Nate!"

"Shit!" That came from Coke, and he could hear Nate screaming, "Hey! Hey!" to get the bull's attention. Coke bounced off him, and there was Fred, the Aussie digging in next to him to shield him from the bull's horn.

Okay. Okay, focus on keeping your feet under you. As soon as you pop free, run the other way. Listen to Dillon. Keep your goddamn feet under you.

The jolt when his hand came free shook him to his toes, and he went down, his feet moving even as he hit the dirt.

"Down, Jason!" That was Dill again, and he did the stop, drop and roll, arms over his head.

He felt the wind, then the impact as the bull's hooves hit the dirt next to his head. So he skittered the other way.

"Run! Run, Jase! Straight ahead!"

He was trying, but he wasn't sure which direction that actually was. So he just dug in with his bootheels and pushed, sprinting toward where he hoped Dillon wanted him to go.

The impact of the bull's hooves on his lower back sent him flying into the fence, and his entire body rattled.

Then one of the bullfighters was lifting him, hands on his vest, heaving him up the rails until someone else caught him under the arms and yanked him over.

"Wave at the crowd, buddy." That was Cotton.

He waved, his entire lower body tingling. "She still preggers?"

"Still." Cotton hauled him up and over, then Aje was there too.

"Ninety-five, man. Good ride."

"Get me out of here before Doc..."

"Before I what? You okay, Jason?" *Oh fuck*. Fuck, he couldn't fool Doc too many more times.

He held out his casted wrist. "How's it looking?"

The guys kept him on his feet.

"I'll need you back in sports medicine." There was a long pause. "Someone get Jason his dark glasses. His eyes are having a hard time adjusting to the light. I can tell."

Oh, Jesus. He sagged. *Does Doc know? Is he gonna tell?*

"See you in a few, son," Doc said in a tone that brooked no argument.

"I need Bax."

He couldn't do this alone. He needed Bax...and help.

"You got this, Jase. If Doc was going to tell, he would have. Breathe." Dillon's voice was loud in his ear.

"I'm right here, Mini." Bax's hands landed on him, and he could breathe.

He nodded at Bax and Dillon and everyone else, then limped around wherever the heck they were until Bax led him to the hall that led back to sports medicine.

"Breathe, Mini. Here are your glasses."

"Thanks. He knows, Bax."

"He's Doc. He probably has known the whole time. He cain't tell. He's a doctor."

Oh. Oh, right.

"Let him check you out. Maybe try to give you a talking to. Then we move on."

Jason took a deep breath. He could do that.

"Does it hurt?" Bax muttered.

"Tingles. I'm okay. I did good, huh?" Ninety-five was fucking better than good. That meant one more event down. One more check to do improvements on their house.

"Yep. One day closer to the finals, babe."

Doc swept in seconds after they made it to sports medicine. "Back here, Jason."

Bax took him to a curtained-off area, he thought, from the sound of the metal rings on a bar.

"Okay, we're the only ones back here. How bad are your eyes, Jason?"

"I—" What was he supposed to say? "The bull hit my back, Doc."

"I know. Take off your shirt and I'll look at that and your wrist. I'm not going to give you a hard time, but I need to know."

"You've seen the scans, Doc," Bax said.

"Mmm." Doc prodded at his back. "So it's all gone. Do you understand how fucking dangerous this is?"

"I got this. Just through the finals. Please. Just through the finals."

Doc came around to turn his wrist this way and that. "I'll tell you what I told Sam Bell. I advise against it. However, I'll let it go until the end of this season. If it goes past the finals, I'll have to talk to Ace. Believe it or not, I do understand."

"I bought a house. Me and Andy Baxter. We bought a house. I need to win the finals." He needed that win.

"I hear you. I don't like it. You've got eight events left. That's twenty-four rides before the finals. That's harsh." Doc touched his back again, and he hissed. "Jonesy, get the ice."

"Keep it together, Jase." Dillon's voice was soft. "You got this."

Right. Confident. Sure. He had this. He wasn't worried. He knew how to ride. "Gonna have a bruise, huh, Doc?"

"And how."

Jonesy whistled. "You start peeing blood, you come back in."

"Will do." Like he'd know. He wasn't going to stress. The touch of the ice was like heaven and hell all at once, and he panted a little. "Did I break the cast?"

"No. You got lucky, Jason." Now Doc sounded back to normal, all bark-y and stuff. "Don't get hung up."

"Right. I'm on it." His heart raced, and he wanted to puke. Fuck him, he was tired, his adrenaline running out and just bringing pain with it.

"Come on, Mini. Let's head back to the hotel. I'll make him rest, Doc." Bax sounded as blown out as he felt.

"I want that ice on him. Jonesy, give him a shot. I want him sleeping. When do you head out, Andy? Are you flying or driving?"

"We're just going to the hotel tonight, then driving out tomorrow." Bax was still touching his good arm. "Is it that bad?"

"Nah. Nah, it's just tingling," he lied. "I got this."

"If I give you some pills for later, will you take them?" Jonesy asked.

"Sure, man. I just want to go get supper and chill." Sundays were early. He didn't have to stress it.

"Good deal. I'll take your word."

"Be safe, son," Doc said, then he was moving on.

"See?" Dillon murmured in his ear. "All good."

"Turning you off now," he told Dillon.

"Oh, every day, Jase."

Fucker.

Jason wanted to reach for Bax, hold his hand, but he couldn't. He knew that. "I need to go now."

"I'm going to get the truck. Someone will come get you and help you out."

Wait. Was Bax mad? Had he done something wrong?

"Sure." He'd just sit here and be blind.

Bax was gone before he could even think what or how to ask, and Jonesy was still humming some tuneless thing, but Doc was working on one of the Brazilians, it sounded like.

He stayed put, and it wasn't long before Coke was there, freshly showered. "I told Andy I'd help you get to the truck. How bad is it?"

"Not bad." Nothing he wouldn't leave in sports medicine.

"Good deal. Come on." Coke was always willing to take him at his word, but he almost made a lie of it when he slid off the exam table. *Shit.*

"Ah." Coke grabbed the back of his jeans, hauling him upright. "Gotcha. Let's try a few steps."

"Who's watching?" He didn't want this to get worse.

"Me. I got your ice pack. Walk."

He managed a few steps. Each one felt like he was stepping on knives. He knew it wasn't permanent, knew it was swelling back there, but damn, it was scary. Just as scary now as it had been the first time it had happened.

"Just out to loading now," Coke said. "Then you're golden, huh?"

"That's me. End of the fucking rainbow." He did it by grinding his teeth until he thought his jaw would pop.

"You're a little green like a leprechaun." And there was Dillon. "You ride with the boys, babe. I'll follow y'all to the hotel."

"Sure thing." Coke got him into Bax's truck where he could stretch out in the back, then the doors all closed. "Good to go, Andy."

"You're gonna let the clown drive your vehicle?" Bax asked.

"He has his own set of keys."

Jason chuckled, praying that Bax didn't hit a lot of bumps.

Bax was damn quiet, but he did drive careful, easing them out into traffic, which was always a bear after events.

"You going to be able to eat supper, Jase?" Coke asked, and he nodded, because otherwise Gramps wouldn't leave him alone. "I want a baked potato or something."

"That sounds good. Maybe I'll just have some fries." Something he could eat with his uninjured hand.

"Finger food," Bax murmured, and he had to strain to hear it. What the hell?

Goddamn it, why did Gramps have to be here? If they were gonna snarl, they damn sure needed to have it over and done with. He didn't want them to be all quiet and not talking to each other.

They got to the hotel, and Coke seemed to know all of a sudden, gently touching his shoulder. "We'll be up for dinner. I'll wait down here for Dillon. AJ wanted to come too."

"Half an hour," Bax snapped before hustling him to the elevator.

He kept his lips tight all the way up, down the hall, and until the door lock clicked. "What the fuck is wrong?"

Bax exploded. "Goddamn it, Mini. You could have been cut in half! That fucking bull had your goddamn number! I lost ten years off my life."

"I kept my feet under me!" He could holler too. "I did everything right!"

"Your body might know what to do, but you're already hurt. Jesus, Jase! What are you gonna do if you get kicked in the head again? I cain't take this."

What the fuck was wrong with Bax? He knew that this was what they did. Cowboys rode and they got hurt when they fell off.

"Jason. We got our own place now. We can just go home. Just quit." Bax moved close but didn't touch.

"The finals are coming, Bax. I could win the year." It could happen.

"That's still eight events away! Even if you took a few off…"

He reached out, whacking Bax with his cast by accident. "Andy Baxter, I am a cowboy. I ain't gonna lie down and die. I'll heal up."

"What if you catch your head again? What if it knocks you senseless? What if—"

Jason growled. "Dammit. What if, what if, what if? I cain't live like that! I got to do this!"

"Why? What the fuck is so important about the fucking finals?"

"Because I said I'd do it. Because that was what I swore!" And he didn't know what happened after that. He didn't know what worth he'd have. If he could do this—this one big thing—then maybe the fact that there was fifty plus years of not knowing and being in the fucking dark looming would be okay.

"Jesus, Mini." Bax sat on the bed, the squeak telling Jason he'd just flopped down. "I'm scairt. That's it, right there. I'm afraid you're gonna get killed."

"You know as well as I do that's a thing." He made his way over, easing himself down. "I got to try. It's the only thing I know how to do, and if I win…"

"What's the chance of that? Cotton's on your ass, Eduardo, Kynan—you got to be damn near perfect."

"Then I'll be damn near perfect." Ninety-five. He'd ridden today for an eighty-six and a ninety-five. That was as close to perfect as he could ask for.

"But—"

"No buts," he said firmly. "I got one chance, and we got the best team ever. Coke, Dill, Nattie, Emmy. Hell, Cotton would turn out for me, even though I'd never ask him to. And I need you on my side."

"I am." Bax took his good hand in one of his. "Always. Just hate seeing you get kicked around."

"I wasn't having fun, that's for fucking sure. My back is killing me."

"Let me get you another ice pack. You want to clean up? I'll order some supper when Coke and them get up if they come before you get out of the shower. I can wrap up your cast." Bax was babbling now.

"Kiss me." *Tell me you've got my back, Bax.*

Bax pulled him around a tiny bit and kissed him long and slow, like he meant every brush of lips and tongue against his. "I love you, Jason Scott. Don't you forget that."

"I won't. I never do. I'm riding for us. For forever, you know."

"I know." Bax leaned against him for a little bit, then sighed. "Okay, let's get all that dirt and bull goo off you."

"Yeah. Gross." He let Bax ease him up to sitting. "Ninety-five points, man."

"It was a hell of a ride, Mini." Bax sounded much better. He probably needed to eat too. "That bull is gonna hurt someone."

"I bet they retire him to stud after this season." Jason had no idea who owned that one, but most of their contractors knew when it was time to get a bull out of rotation. Bodacious had set a precedent for head bashers back in the day. "I'd have been okay if it wasn't for my damn cast."

"Uh-huh. Get in the shower, Mini. You stink."

He chuckled, letting Bax tape his cast up in plastic, then getting into the shower to scrub up. The world had righted itself again, and Coke and them would be up for supper. Like always. Some things were eternal.

He fell off. He got the fuck back on.

Chapter Twenty

Bax stood out by the truck. They were loaded and ready to go to New Orleans, but he couldn't make himself open the damn door. His hands felt cold, and he was sweating. He thought maybe this was what a panic attack felt like.

Jason came out, following the rope system they'd set up to the carport, his casted hand held up against his chest real careful-like.

Jesus, he was still beat to hell.

The wrist wasn't the half of it. Jase's back was bruised from shoulder blades to ass, just black still, and he knew Jason wasn't sleeping right with it. Mini wasn't ready to go back, and Bax knew it.

"You okay?" Jason asked, and he shook his head violently.

"Let's sit this one out, Jason. Just this event. Let you heal up. Make Doc happy."

"What? We're all packed up."

That wasn't a no. That *so* wasn't a no.

"I know. But it ain't too late to call a medical. Compromise with me. Take this week off and I won't bitch for two events."

Jason frowned and began working his way around the truck, one hand trailing along the vehicle on his way over to Bax.

Shit. Bax knew he was being a little bit of a freak about this, but he couldn't help it. Jason was still pale. Hurtin'.

"Hey." He said it when Jason got close, waiting to see what his stubborn man was gonna do.

"Hey." Jase walked right into his space, reaching for his face, touching him intimately—smoothing his eyebrows, tracing the lines on his forehead, thumbs tracing his lips. He knew Jason was looking, reading his expression.

Bax had to admit it. He was stressed.

"You think I cain't do it?" Jason asked.

"I think you can do any damn thing you try, but you need a break. You need to heal up. The finals are more important than the season, even with the newer points system." That was the solid truth.

"Part of me wants to fight and tell you to get in the damn truck." Jase was still touching. "A bigger part of me is tired and wants to go pick out one of them blow-up hot tub deals. Tell me I'm not being a pussy."

"Nope. You're being smart, Mini, and I ain't just saying that." Bax turned things over in his brain for a minute. "If you wasn't blind, but you had the injuries you have right now, and the season you've been having, what would you do?"

"Stay home. I'm gonna have another crash. I'm not in the middle."

Bax felt a little like screaming—and not in that bad way, but rejoicing because he knew his Jase, dammit, and because he was fixin' to get his way without Jason whaling on his happy ass.

Jesus, when did we grow up?

Bax took a deep breath, then let it out. "So we stay home this time and do the smart thing. Hell, we don't and someone like Ace will wonder why you're desperate."

"You'll make burgers?"

Okay. Okay, Jase was going to be chill, so he was too. They could just stay home, breathe. Rest.

He took Jason's hand, heading back into the house. "I will. And baked potatoes later." They both loved those. He'd unload the truck in a bit.

"Sounds good. I want the six-person blow-up hot tub with the drink holders."

"You got it. I'll call that feller we took the card from." They'd talked to a million people in town already.

"Good deal." They headed back together, the lines around Jason's mouth already easing.

Thank God. He'd made the right call. One more week to heal. They were gearing up for the finals, and he knew it. Post break, they always barreled through the events to the big show.

This time, it was different.

This time, it was literally winner take all.

Chapter Twenty-One

"Jason! Goddamn it, Jason Scott, we got to talk!" Ace was shouting at him.

Jason stopped, jaw set tight. "Go on, Bax. I got this."

"Jase…"

"Go on."

"I'll walk him back out, Andy." Dillon's voice was sure in his ear.

Bax reluctantly left, because that was what he would do, and it would look weird as hell if he stayed to hold Jason's hand just to talk to Ace.

He turned, his dark glasses pushed up. "What you need, man?"

"You've been avoiding me, son." Ace was front and center, so he tried to 'look'.

"Why? I got nothing to avoid. I just been trying to stay healthy." That was the truth. Sorta. "What's up?"

"Jason! *Bom dia*! That was a good ride, sim? So good?" Balta's voice filled the tunnel, the sound of the man's hand clapping on Ace's shoulder like a shot.

"Balta and Raul are there. Raul's right at your shoulder. Joao is still out, remember." Thank God for the clown.

"Hey, guys. Ace was just about to dress me down." He grinned, rolling his shoulders and bouncing on his toes.

"I wasn't— I just wanted to make contact, dammit. I haven't seen you since the accident."

"Bah." Raul's voice was soft, but sure. "Always here. Jason rides always."

Fuck yeah.

"Well, I ain't seen him." Ace's drawl deepened. He and Balta loved each other, but man could they bump chests, and Ace always took Raul's little insubordinations out on Balta. It was kinda great.

"Sorry, Boss," Jason said. "Really. I'm doing right by the association, yeah?"

"Suck up," Dillon whispered, and Jason fought to keep a straight face.

"You're doing fine, Jason. I just wanted to put eyes on you. What does Doc say about your new injuries?"

Jason fought again, this time not to roll his eyes, which he knew he still did. Ace knew damn well what Doc thought. He met with the man daily.

"I'm right as rain. Leave it all in sport medicine, you know?" *Fuck right off, boss. You don't get to make that call.*

"Well, all right then. You just keep your mind in the middle."

He wondered if Ace knew. He really did. The man walked a fine line between cowboys and corporate, but he did try to have their backs.

Still, once it was out, he'd have to quit, so he was admitting nothing.

Raul and Balta moved Jason off down the hall, the huge Brazilians about as subtle as, well, Bax.

"Thanks, y'all. You were welcome as the rain in spring."

"Ace smells things on the air," Balta said. "Like a hound dog. I will always help if I can."

"I appreciate it. How's Joao, man?"

"He is in therapy. The riding, it is done for him, I think. For me too. Raul can ride for all of us."

"Damn." Joao had been like Sammy—great if he rode, hurt as hell if he didn't.

"He's sad, but he will do well raising horses, I think." Raul's English was probably as good as it would get now, but Jason was pretty proud of him for trying so hard.

"Did you hear we bought a house in Corpus? On the water. Y'all should come."

"Oh, we should! Did you get a hot tub?" Balta did love anything that soothed his poor back.

Jason chuckled, and there was Bax, the smell of Stetson and Irish Spring like home. "We did. Seats six. And there's a little suite with a sitting area and a kitchenette deal for visitors."

"Well, then, you tell us when we can come, and we will."

Bax chuckled, a hand on Jason's back. "We even got one of them adjustable medical beds, man. How about after Billings? We got two weeks between there and KC."

"We'll come. We will make *feijoada* and laugh together." Balta sounded tickled.

"I'm in," Jason said. "As long as Raul makes that salad with the hearts of whatever."

"Palm," Raul said, laughter in his voice. "Thank you for inviting us, amigo."

"You know it. I'll text you all the address and stuff, so y'all have it. We'll have fun."

Shit, the Brazilians were a hoot and a half, and Joao could translate.

"We will. Doc is coming, huh? Run."

Jason laughed, but he did just that, Bax guiding him toward the exit.

"One more event down. We did it."

"We did. That was a good ride, babe, just like Balta said. You were way more solid." Bax sounded proud and a tiny bit relieved.

"Yeah. I'm feeling less like I got trampled now." Handy, given that he had been less stepped on this week.

"Imagine that. Your balance was way better."

"Cool." He took out his earpiece once they got to the truck. No sense in Dillon hearing everything they said in private. "I stink. I swear to God, Bax. I didn't used to stink so bad after work."

"I think you just notice shit more, Mini. I think you smell fine." Bax took his hand for a moment.

"Oh, maybe. I don't know." He guessed it had to be at least a little real, right? That idea that other senses got all sharper and shit? He sure felt like he could hear every damn noise at the new house, and he had to put on the TV sometimes to drown it out. Thank God Bax could sleep through any damn thing.

"You handled Ace okay?"

Jason nodded. He thought so. He hoped so. "I had help from the guys."

The story of his fucking life. He would do his best to return the favor. He'd already made a donation to the rider help fund in Joao's name…

"Where'd you go?" Bax asked. "You here with me?"

"Yeah. Yeah, I'm here. I was thinking about how the guys help me out."

"They're good friends." Bax paused, and Jason heard a jaw-cracking yawn. "And some of them are just returning the favor, mind. Remember when Balta broke his shoulder? Who did he have then?"

Jason snorted. He'd spent two weeks in a hotel in Dallas right after Balta had gotten out of the hospital, doing Balta's therapy exercises with him until a spot opened up at a sports rehab place. That man could curse fluently in both Portuguese and English.

"We do what we got to." He let out a long breath. "Do you think Ace guessed?"

"Nah, he'd pull you. They got all insurance and stuff."

"Yeah." Now he could inhale again. "Yeah, okay. I just need Doc to stay quiet."

"As long as you're winning, he will. He knows better than anyone what's at stake here." Bax reached over to hold his hand again.

"Eh, I ain't getting any blinder."

Bax snorted, because they both knew that wasn't exactly true. His eyes worked fine. It was the connection between brain and eyeballs that didn't work. It was one of the reasons he figured shit out so easy.

It could be a lot worse, he guessed. Some days that meant something. Others, not so much.

But he knew Bax worried. It wouldn't take much. It never did. Sam Bell had proved that. Sammy had taken that horn for Beau, and—Sam was never going to be okay again.

Sam was home, Beau had him, but the Sammy they'd known was someone else now.

He guessed he was too. Maybe they all were.

Bulls left their mark.

Bax hummed along with the music, and they both jumped a mile when Bax's phone rang, Garth's *Rodeo* blaring.

"Can you get that, babe?"

"Surely." He tapped the bottom of the phone, sliding his finger. He got it, nine times out of ten. "'Lo?"

"We're heading to the hospital with Em. Her water broke." Dillon chuckled softly, and the sound was pure evil. "All over Ace."

"Oh fuck." *Talk about poetic goddamn justice*. "Cotton with y'all?"

"He's taking his truck. Coke just carried her. Total panic mode. Cotton was a little out of his league."

"Oh. Do y'all need help?" Bax asked, and Jason tilted his head. What were they supposed to do, exactly? Helping pregnant ladies pop them out wasn't in their repertoire.

"Well, y'all could call Cotton. He's freaking out, and that way he can have some company on the drive." Dillon was chuckling. They heard the GPS talking, then Coke. "I got this, babe. You just hold on."

"Holding. Breathe, Emmy-girl, and cross your legs." Coke's voice was as dry as dust.

Jason barked out a sharp laugh. "Right on. Calling Cotton."

"Good deal. We'll keep you posted."

"We'll be at the hotel," Bax said.

They hung up with Dillon, and he hit the button so Bax could tell his phone, "Call Cotton."

"She squirted on Ace, y'all. On Ace!"

Wow, not even a hello. "Coke's got her. She's in good hands."

"Bullshit. She should be in my hands. Those babies are mine." Okay, little fierce Cotton was adorable.

"She will be. You know Gramps. He just does shit." Jason grinned, but only because Cotton couldn't see him.

"You just focus on getting to the hospital in one piece," Bax added.

"Yeah. I told her not to work this event. I told her she was the size of a goddamn house! *'I'll be fine,'* she says. *'You worry too much, Cotton,'* she says."

They both chuckled. "She's a stubborn one," Jason murmured. "She's gonna be bossing those docs and nurses around, no problem."

"You know it." Bax snorted. "Then you got the clown."

Cotton sighed. "You have no idea. None. He threw her baby shower. It was Monster High themed."

"What's a Monster High?" Jason imagined a Frankenstein smoking a doobie.

"The dolls. Like Barbie, but they're vampires and shit."

"That clown freaks me out," Bax teased.

Vampire Barbies…whoa. That was…for a baby?

"I'm guessing they're girls?" he asked.

"No. No, they're boys." Cotton sighed. "Okay, I've got to park. Thanks, guys. I'll keep you posted."

"Holler if you need anything." Like they would. Coke and Dillon were in their element, for fuck's sake, and he would bet AJ was on his way to the hospital. That man was stupid for babies.

"I will. Later, y'all." Cotton hung up, and Bax started to chuckle.

"Lord have mercy, that man is in for it."

Jason nodded. "You know it. We're going to have many nieces and nephews..."

Between that, dogs and horses, they were gonna be busy.

He liked busy. A lot. That would keep him from thinking, for sure.

Hell, being busy and loving life was what they were here for, right? He sure hoped so. If not, then he was doing all this shit wrong.

Chapter Twenty-Two

Bax took a deep breath, taking Jason's arm as they left the elevator to head out to the arena.

It was the first day of the finals, and the lobby was bustling with riders, staff and fans.

"Okay, Dillon," he heard Jason murmur. "We're in the lobby."

"On my way." Dillon was right there across the way. "Ace is off to your left, doing an impromptu interview with the *Rodeo News*, so skim to your right, toward the coffee shop."

Jason's nostrils flared, and Mini turned them before he did, which was cool. However, Jase ran them right into Kynan, which was less.

"Careful, Scott. You don't want to get hurt before the bulls."

"Fuck off, kid."

"Yeah, yeah. I'm gunning for you, man."

"From nearly eight thousand points behind?" Bax scoffed, easing Jason to his other side. "Dream on."

"I heard y'all bought a house together. Are you gonna go make little cowboys?"

Jason's fists balled up, and suddenly Beau Lafitte was right there, getting in between them. "Back on up, now. I know you don't want to be making trouble in front of Ace, chile."

Kynan scoffed. "Whatever." He stalked off, his long legs making distance.

"Nice one." Bax clapped Beau on the back. "Thanks."

"Anytime. You been on fire, cher. You did good."

Jason beamed at Beau's praise. "Thanks, Bobo. I appreciate it."

"You're welcome. You just stay out of Kynan's way, huh? He's got him a mad-on."

"Poor little fuckhead," Bax rolled his eyes. He was a goddamn cowboy, not an 'athlete' like Kynan. He'd clean the little fucker's plow.

"He'll grow up…eventually."

"Who? Bax?" That was AJ, chortling.

He flipped Aje off, but Jase cracked up, howling with happy laughter.

"Y'all all suck," Bax stated.

That just sent them all off laughing again.

"What's funny?" Dillon asked, and Beau popped off.

"Bax's sucking."

"Oh. Out here in public?" Dillon waggled his eyebrows. The guys formed a little flanking type guard around him and Jason, moving them toward the exit, which kept everyone else away.

"Y'all be nice," Jason chuckled. "Seriously, you don't want to be banned from the new house."

"Jase! You got an all-new house with the ocean!" Sam Bell clapped Jason on the shoulder. "Good on you."

"We did. It's real nice. Got one of them adjustable beds in the guest room."

"Yeah, because I paid for it," Dillon said, snorting.

"No one asked you to, Dillweed." Not that Dillon was really complaining. Bax knew that.

"Nope. It was for my bullfighter. Who needs coffee?"

"I do." They all said it. Lord, they were a coffee-loving bunch, as long as none of them made it.

Bax and Jason got themselves sat with Aje, Coke and Beau, while Dillon and Sammy went for coffee.

"You look healthier, Jase. Seriously." AJ bobbed his head like Jase could see him.

"Thanks." Mini traced circles on the table. "I'm almost healed up. A few more rides, and I'm golden, right?"

"You know it. It's almost statistically impossible for anyone to catch you. Raul and Kynan could get close if you flopped, but I ain't sure they could." Beau was damn proud of Jason, Bax thought.

"I'll make sure they can't. I need this." There was a ferocity in Mini's face, a harsh need.

"You've always been able to get what you set your mind to," AJ said quietly. "We're here for you this year, buddy. Just you. Ain't none of us worried about ourselves."

"I appreciate y'all, more than I can say. I want my title, then I want to go home."

Bax loved that—how Mini was focused on home, on their crazy house on the ocean, on building their lives together.

He wanted that too. This whole event year had been a freaking roller coaster, and he was sick with worry right now. They just had a few more rides.

But those few more rides were on the rankest bulls, with the biggest crowds. With every suit who owned and ran the league right there, front and center.

Christ.

"You're all tense," Jason muttered, rubbing shoulders with him. "Stop thinking so hard."

"Gotcha, babe." Bax took a deep, deep breath, then let it out. It was going to be what it was, right?

"This is what we've been fighting for. This event." Coke's lips were tight, and Bax didn't think the old man was going to be fighting bulls much longer. There was a sorrow in Coke now, an exhaustion.

Gramps had seen too much, taken too many hits.

It made him sad, because it was going to be the end of an era—not when Jase retired. They were all going that way—but when Coke did.

Dillon came back with the first round of coffees, and he leaned on Coke gently for a moment. "We got this, guys." Dillon was always upbeat. Relentless.

"Yes." Sam nodded, gave him a crooked smile. "Time to be champs—you and Boug."

Jason nodded, mouth firm. "It's my year, damn it."

Bax prayed then. Silently, but sure as anything. *Please God, let it be true. Let him get through. Let us go home.*

That was all he wanted in all the world.

To take a whole and healthy Jason Scott home.

So they would take this finals one day at a time, one ride at a time. Bax would hold Jason on by the power of will alone, if he had to.

Starting today.

Chapter Twenty-Three

"Okay, Jase. This one will break your neck if you let him. Don't let him." That was Gramps. "You done rode five. You got this."

"I won't," he muttered.

"I can't wait for you to meet the babies," Cotton said. The man held his vest, talking nonsense to him. "Two little boys. Well, they ain't little. They were both over seven pounds. Emmy was pissed."

Jason felt the bull crouch, and felt Bax move him with one booted foot. Bax was on the gate, making sure the bull was in the right place. Beau was doing Bax's usual job of pulling his rope.

"Come on, you bastard. Stand up!" Bax sounded worried, but Jason wasn't. He wanted the good bulls. Bax was gonna get him an ulcer, acting like he was.

"Okay, he's up." Bax was away, and now it was Beau jabbering at him, reminding him to keep his eyes open, his arm up, his chest out.

Then Jason nodded.

Head up.

One.

Eyes open.

Two.

Spurring.

Three.

Fuck, he was sliding.

Four.

Into the well. *Correct! Correct, dammit.*

Five.

Eyes open.

Six.

Hold on, you asshole!

Seven.

Jason heard the buzzer, and he let go, knowing that he was going to have a bad get off. He could hear it in Dillon's panicked voice, shouting at him to cover his head. He put his arms up around his helmet, which meant he landed hard on his tailbone, jarring his whole body, stealing his breath.

"Get up, Jase! Move!"

"I'm trying!" He tried to clear his head, keep it down. The jolt as the bull's hoof clipped his helmet and rang his damn bell.

His bell.

Sammy.

Lord, that was funny.

Except it wasn't, and he rolled, but he chose the wrong way and a horn clipped his shoulder.

"Hey! Hey, bull. Hey!" Coke was just bellowing, and someone not a bull kicked him in the ribs, so he knew one of the bullfighters was actually clinging to the bull.

"Jason! Listen to me, goddammit!" Dillon's voice was sharp as a knife. "Crawl forward. Fast. I'll grab you."

Whoa. It must be bad if the clown was risking himself and Coke's fury.

Jason got to his knees, getting a swift kick in the hip for his trouble. That spun him in a half circle to his left, and he tried to correct, scrambling as Dillon shouted more directions.

Please God. Please. I need to get out.

He felt Dillon's hands straightening him up, dragging him to the camera cage in the center of the arena.

He belly flopped on it, catching his thighs on the metal, and he grunted when Dillon yanked him the rest of the way up. He felt the breeze as the bull went by, the cursing and whomp of a twirling rope from Adam Taggart as the pick-up man went flying past.

Fuck, he was dizzy and queasy, and he wanted to go back to the hotel and hide. Now. He wasn't sure how he was going to get down, much less how he was going to get out.

"We got this, Jase. Don't panic." Dillon's voice echoed in his ear and around him, the whisper there and gone as Dillon stood up and turned on his arena mic. "Safe!"

Don't panic. Right. He felt wetness on his face, and he reached up, finding it sticky. That wasn't syrup. Jesus. His ears rang for a minute, and he thought he might puke.

Then Bax and AJ were there.

"Let's cheer Jason on!" yelled David Donaldson, the arena announcer for the crowd behind him as Bax and AJ half carried him out. *Guess that's the way to go, so I look injured and not blind.*

"Don't let Doc get a hold of me."

"Too late!" Jonesy was so damn perky. "Let me get the bleeding stopped."

"You ain't Doc," he teased, relieved. Then he sat back and let Jonesy work on him. If he sat real still and was super quiet, maybe he could stop wanting to hurl.

"You pass out at all?"

"Nope." Not even a second. That might have been a blessing.

"Okay." Jonesy poked and prodded until he wanted to scream. AJ had left, but he could hear Bax, his breathing tense.

"You done? I need to go, man." He wanted a shower and a little quiet. His head was banging.

"I would like for you to get a CAT scan, Jason," Jonesy said quietly. "Your helmet is cracked and that scalp laceration is pretty big."

"Nope. I'm good. Plaster my happy ass up." He wasn't going anywhere.

"After the finals," Bax said. "Once it's done, Jonesy."

Jonesy sighed. "Okay. Two shakes." His voice went a little distant. "I don't like it, Jason. At all."

"I got tomorrow left. Just let it go."

"Head injuries don't just let go."

No. No, he knew from head injuries. Wasn't like he had to worry about blurry vision. He woulda laughed if it didn't hurt so much.

"I'm good, Jonesy. I just want to go have a cold Coke and a burger." God, that was a lie. He couldn't eat right now for love or money.

He'd puke his guts out.

"Well, you're all patched up. I recommend something easy on the stomach and bedrest until you have to ride again. Nothing that will jostle your poor brain in your skull."

"Right on. I'll see you tomorrow, y'all. Thanks." He got up, the universe feeling like it was moving under his feet.

Bax took his arm, and that didn't even have to look like the weirdo leading the blind. He needed a steady hand, and Jonesy knew it.

He was in the truck in no time, Bax like a stone beside him. He didn't say a word, and he didn't have to, because Bax's phone started ringing.

"Hey, Momma."

"Is he okay?"

Jesus fucking Christ. "I'm fine, Momma."

"You got your bell rung. I saw it." Her voice stayed even, but he could hear the worry. The hint of accusation.

"Yeah, but I didn't get knocked out or nothing. Two more rides, Momma. Just tomorrow." Just tomorrow and he was golden.

"You be careful. None of it matters if you get killed, son."

He gritted his teeth. "Yes, ma'am."

"I love you." She sounded resigned now. She'd been around roughstock men her whole life. She knew he'd made up his mind to ride.

"Andy? Are you okay?"

"I'll be fine, Miz Scott." So formal. Bax was mad.

"I love you too, son. You'll be in your own bed, day after tomorrow."

"I can't wait. Love you." Bax lightened up some for his momma, but it was an effort. Jason could feel how stiff his arm was.

They hung up, and he just closed his eyes and floated, letting himself feel the music in his bones.

"You cain't go to sleep, Mini," Bax murmured. Not mean or nothin'. Just low and worried.

"Okay. 'm awake." *Don't be pissed at me, Bax. I'm so damn tired and so close.*

"Good. I got to keep you that way for a few hours, all right? We're almost to the hotel, but we'll go in through self-park and go right up that back elevator." Bax's voice was actually kinda soothing, so if he had a mad-on, he was hiding it well.

"Sounds like one hell of a plan."

"Good deal. You gonna get all urpy if I order some food?" Bax knew him well.

"No. I probably need to eat something. French fries, maybe?"

"Sounds good. Anything else hurt? Jonesy didn't check anything but your head."

"I'm just tenderized. I'd make a great chicken fried steak right now." Shit, he was funny.

Bax snorted, and Jason felt the tension ease some. "You would. Your scrambled brains can be gravy."

Oh, ew. "That's borderline gross, man. I approve."

"Thank you. I try." Bax chuckled. "You gonna live over there?"

"Are you kidding? I got two more rides before I announce."

"I know. I know, which is why I'm keeping my mouth shut." Bax made a wry noise. "It ain't easy."

"I know." Two more rides. That was it. He could manage. Two more. Even if he had to duct tape his head onto his shoulders to do it. Bax would just have to suck it up.

Which he knew Bax would do for him.

"I love you." He reckoned Bax knew, but more than that, he figured Bax needed to hear it.

"Love you, Mini. I really do." Bax finally touched his arm, and he could breathe. He knew it was all right.

"I know. We're checking out in the morning, driving from the end of the finals? We can make it to Vegas, maybe, spend the night, go home."

"Yeah. Yeah, we can do that. I'll drive half dead, so we can just go home."

Jason knew how Bax felt. Home, home, home.

"Yeah. Go home. Soak. Sleep. Eat hot dogs." Park the truck for a few months. "We going to see Momma for Thanksgiving?"

"Her and Jack are coming to ours. Coke and the clown too. We'll go to Coke's next year." Bax chuckled, the sound soft. "Beau and Sammy want us for Christmas."

"Cool." Look at his man, settling down. Jason was ready to settle in and do…almost anything else. His bones were tired. Hell, his everythings were tired, when he got right down to it.

"Don't go to sleep, Mini. We're almost there."

"M'okay." He was feeling so muzzy, but he sat up a little, trying to do as he'd been told.

"Uh-huh. I will take you to the ER if you don't even out. Your momma has my number."

"Shut up." He would rather have Doc than the ER. Christ.

"Well, you can't ride like this, Jase." They pulled into the parking lot. He could hear the sound of the grate to the parking structure.

"Good thing I got a few hours."

"Yeah." The truck stopped. "We're two spaces from the elevator. We got back fast."

"Okay. You coming around?" *Please?*

"I am. I won't just leave you out here." Now Bax was laughing at him, but that was okay. That was better than mad.

"Butthead. I will puke on your shoes." Out of pure adoration, of course.

"No way. I wore my Lucheses today." Bax eased him out of the cab of the truck, hands hard and steady.

"Mmm…I like how those make your butt tight."

"Now he perks up. Just took my butt. I got my earpiece in still, but I think everyone is still at the show. You just put one foot in front of the other." Bax got him in the elevator.

He leaned and swallowed hard as it went up. "Lord, I'm tired."

"I got you. Just lean on me, babe."

Story of his life, right there.

Bax had him. All he had to do was let it happen. Jason swallowed hard against the nausea, glad when the world stopped moving. Bax led him to their room, and he sat with a groan.

"Let's get you in the shower, babe. You're covered in blood. I need to get it off your chaps."

"Just— I need to sit a minute. Get the water going."

"Okay." Bax kissed the corner of his lips.

He sat there for a second, trying to remember how to breathe. In and out. In and out. One breath, then another. He head pounded like one of them monkey toys that clapped the cymbals. He might just puke for real, now that Bax's boots were out of the way.

He leaned back, trying hard not to cry, because damn, he wanted to.

"Hey." Bax was there again, easing off his boots, unbuckling his chaps.

"I'm sorry, Bax." He just couldn't make himself move.

"I know. You gotta get through it. I get it." Bax helped him up, his hands gentle. "The shower is hot, but not too steamy. Don't want you getting sick or getting a bleed."

"I just… I'm so tired. Seriously. I want to go home so bad, but I can't. I have to do this." He let Bax lead him, knowing that he had diarrhea of the mouth. This sucked— Why couldn't he stay healthy? What else was riding going to take from him?

"Two more rides, then we're on the road. Doc set us up with that guy in Corpus, and we'll see him, huh?" Bax was the reasonable one now, which just made him laugh.

"You know it. Two more, then it's over."

"No, Mini. No. Two more, then it starts."

He closed his eyes and swayed. "From your lips to God's ears."

"I love you." Bax folded him into the gentlest hug ever.

"I know. I count on it."

Two more rides. He had this.

Chapter Twenty-Four

There was no fucking way Jason was riding again. The son of a bitch had puked all goddamn night, he was barely walking straight—and he'd already missed the first round today. It was over.

"I'm riding in the short go, Bax."

Coke nodded. "He has to, to clench the championship. He don't have to ride good, but he has to ride. He does the eight, and it's all she wrote."

"But—"

"Statistically, Kynan or Raul could still edge him out, Andy." That was Dillon, who had been an accountant and knew his numbers. "But not if he rides."

"Goddammit!" Bax hit the rail with one hand.

"I'm riding."

"You cain't."

Jason's lips firmed, his chin lifting. "Watch me. We didn't risk all this for second place."

"Mini."

"Stop it," Dillon snapped. "People are noticing, and the cameras won't be far behind."

Jason wasn't ready to ride. Bax just wanted to scream with frustration.

"My last ride, Bax. I need you behind me."

Jesus, that was blackmail. He wanted to just walk away and say he was sitting his ass in the locker room until this was over. But he couldn't do that.

"You know I'm right here, Mini. You know I am. But I ain't got to like it."

"Nope. Some things are out of our hands."

Jase stood there and waited. He was the last to go, and damn if Raul didn't ride for an eighty-nine, overtaking Jason in the standings.

"Goddamn it."

"It's going to be all right, Bax." Jase was pure-D gray.

"Sure it is." His jaw hurt from clenching it so hard. Kynan was up next, and that son of a bitch was a clutch rider. The bigger the pressure, the better he did.

The little shit did what he said he would too. Eight seconds, spurring and solid, and Bax would be damned if he didn't ride for a ninety-three-eight. "Motherfucker."

"All you got to do is ride. Just make the eight," Dillon said in their ears, and Jason nodded, wincing as he did, and Bax thought he saw a tear on those white-blond eyelashes.

He was gonna lose his shit.

Jason turned those blank eyes to him. "Pull my rope?"

"I'm right here. I got you." How the fuck could he say no? Jason had pulled a big, rawboned bull named

Chiggergrass, and that damn animal was a chute buster. He would try to bash Jason against the bar.

"Good deal."

Beau was there, and so was Sammy—and Sammy knew this. That rattled Texan could talk. "...and we go to the water and have a beer together. We fish the big uns and we make Beau laugh. You make this cow a bitch, and you ride him so hard he cain't breathe no more..."

Bax was glad Sam was taking the talking, because when Jason climbed over the top rail and started to lower his knees down, Chigger went nuts, bucking back and forth in the chute like one of those old spring-loaded ducks in the playground, head down, then up.

"Please," he prayed, and he had no goddamn idea what he was praying for.

"Motherfuck!" Jason's hand got slammed against the chute, and they damn near lost him under the bull's hooves.

"Jesus!" That was Dillon in a rare moment of blasphemy. "Get that bull set!"

Bax knew he was talking to Coke. Gramps and Nate moved in to make the bull stand, and Bax held Jason up in the air, just dangling.

"I got you," he bit out. "I got you, Mini."

"I trust you." And Jason had, over and over. No question.

God, he wanted to tell Jason to quit. Now. But Jason was trusting him. Was basically begging him to keep his head on straight and get them through this. So Bax held on for dear life, then helped Jason settle on the bull again.

They would do this. They would do this and, God help him, they would go pick out their places in the world.

The bull finally stood, snorting and blowing snot, but waiting. Jason slid down on his back and tied his hand into the rope, Bax pulling it down tight like he knew Jason needed, with his wrist as weak as it still was.

"You do it, Jason. You do this and make it all right." Sammy just kept yammering.

Bax got the rope tight enough, Jason wrapped it, and he knew it was time. His gut churned, nausea rising when he saw Jason settling himself, finding his balance.

He leaned down past Sammy's protective arm, his lips close to Jason's ear. "Don't let go, Mini. Don't let go."

"You got my word." Jason nodded his head and spun out, his lips tight and eyes wide open.

Everyone screamed and stomped, encouraging Mini to hold on, but Bax couldn't even breathe. Sam whooped in his ear, and he could hear the Brazilians screaming wildly, but he watched Jason silently, willing his man to stay up and stay on for eight.

The first five were easy, but Mini started to sway before the six, and suddenly Bax found his voice. "Don't you fucking let go, Jason! You ride that goddamn bull!"

Jason's chin lifted, and Bax would be damned if he didn't make the correction and hit the eight.

His knees buckled.

Praise Jesus, Mini had done it. It was over.

He watched Jason try to find the get off, but then he could hear Dillon shouting in his ear, and things started to slide.

"No! Jason. Go to your right. Jump off to your right."

Nattie's familiar, "Hey, hey, hey!" sounded, and Bax knew Coke was on the other side where he couldn't see, waiting to catch and carry Jase if he had to.

Jason turned the wrong way and walked right into the side of the bull, just bang! Coke cried out and ran to grab him, and Bax would be damned if they both didn't hit the bull's shoulder.

Coke caught the horn and went flying, while Mini stood there like he was stunned.

"Goddamn it, Scott!" Nate bellowed. "Move!"

Mini didn't—or he couldn't—and Bax didn't know which one, but he wasn't fucking standing there to find out. He jumped over the fence and onto the arena.

Adam Taggart zoomed past him, his rope swinging.

Bax dug in, getting some momentum going, and he plowed into Jason, carrying him along. They were gonna go down on the arena floor, but Adam was roping that bull. He could hear David Donaldson's play by play.

"Coke!" Dillon's cry snapped out—huge, because it was in his ear, in the air, and he heard the groan of the crowd, then the whump of Coke's body hitting the ground next to them.

Jason moved then, and so did he, covering Coke with their bodies, protecting the man who had saved them a hundred times in a thousand different ways.

The stomp of hooves next to his ear gave him flashbacks to his worst fucking wrecks, but he wasn't leaving Coke and Jason, no sir—not until someone told him it was safe.

"Adam Taggart has a second rope on that bull, folks, and his brother Brian is moving in!"

Nate was screaming at the bull, and the Aussie accent of Fred was right there too, everyone working to get that damn demon bull away from them. It went on forever, and probably lasted all of half a minute.

No one knew better than Bax how fast a whole fucking life could change.

This was enough.

Bull riding had taken as much, maybe more, than it had given him, and he was fucking done. "Gonna take you to the beach," he bit out.

All Mini said was, "Yes."

Nate finally came and laid hands on him. "Get up, Andy. Come on. We need to get Coke to Doc. Jason too." Nate tugged at his arms.

He climbed to his feet, feeling something wet on his shirt, right at his ribs.

"Damn it. You too, mate," Fred said. "You're bleeding. Kicked you good, he did."

"Nate got kicked?" Bax didn't understand. "Someone needs to get Coke on a stretcher."

Dillon was wailing in his ear, trying desperately to wake Coke up.

"No, mate, you got kicked. That's not someone else's blood."

"I'll be okay. Jason, where are you hurt?" Bax pulled away from Fred.

"Get him out of here." He looked over at Ace, who was right there in the arena, hissing the words out. "What the fuck have you assholes done? Get him in the back before the cameras see his eyes."

Bax nodded, stumbling over his own feet to get to Jason. "Mini. Come on. Eyes down. AJ will bring your glasses." Was Jason hurt or was he just stunned? What if his brain was all swole? He took Jason's arm, flicking out his earpiece so he couldn't hear Dillon shouting shit.

"Coming. Eyes down. I got knocked winding." Jase was talking sense. Praise God.

"Come on. We got to get off the floor. They need room to get Coke out."

"Gramps? What happened to him?" Jason let him walk them out. "What happened to Gramps?"

"Quiet. You fucking walk, you stupid little shit."

Jason pulled off his helmet, spinning across to smack Ace right in the chest. "What did you say to me, asshole?"

Ace puffed up and got up in Jason's face. "You just get your ass to the back. You're gonna be lucky if I don't strip you of every fucking event win you've had this season."

"You try it. I didn't cheat. I didn't break one single fucking rule. You fucking try it, and I will sue you and the league until you glow in the dark."

"Come on." Bax said it to both of them, because this was not the time or the place. "Damn it, Coke is hurt, Ace. Get him help."

"It's your fault he's hurt."

"Get out of the way." Doc zoomed by him, the EMTs carrying a stretcher.

"I—" Ace started.

"You listen to me. We get Coke out. You walk out there with me and we have the big check for the cameras. I will then announce my retirement. Otherwise I walk straight out of here to the media. Fair?"

Jesus, when had Jason gotten so goddamn fierce?

Bax reckoned when he'd decided he needed to do this and make their life off it.

"Fuck." Ace stalked ahead of them, and Bax tugged Jason along.

"Your glasses, Jase," AJ said.

"You stay with Gramps, Bax. I'll be right back." Jason took his glasses. "I got this."

"Yeah." What the hell? He wanted to be with Jason, but Doc chugged back with Coke, and he could hear Dillon talking to the crowd. They still had the damn show to end.

Right. Stick with Coke. Sammy was out there, but he saw Beau running to him.

"Come on. Sports medicine."

"Okay. I— What's Jason doing?" He let Beau turn him, guiding him away. Damn it, he wanted to help somehow. Someone.

"Accepting his check. Cowing Ace. Sam's got him. You need to get your belly cleaned up."

"My what?" Bax looked down. "That ain't my blood." He couldn't feel anything.

Beau snorted. "Your shirt's all tore. Just let Jonesy or Shane look at you."

"Okay… I just…"

"Andy." Beau's voice made him stop. "He did it. He won. It's over. No matter what. Jase won. You get to take him home."

"Okay." He swallowed hard, the lump in his throat suddenly huge. "Yeah. Yeah, okay." His ears rang and he got a little lightheaded.

"Come on. We'll get you cleaned up and go see Coke." Beau sighed softly. "I hate this fucking place. I hate it so goddamn bad, man."

Bax blinked. "Sports medicine?"

"No. Reno."

Oh. Oh, shit. Yeah, Sam had been ruined for life here.

"Andy. Sit here." Shane steered him to a gurney. "Shirt off."

He stripped down. "How's Coke?"

Shane shook his head, snapping on gloves. "Ambulance took him for X-rays. He was still out, last I heard. Doc's with him." He got a quick look. "Jason's really blind?"

Bax nodded slowly. No sense lying now. "Yeah. Yeah, since he got hit so bad."

"Jesus, brave, crazy son of a bitch. Good on him. Seriously." Shane wiped him up. "It's not deep. I'll bandage it."

"Thanks." He winced when Shane cleaned out his scratch. Now he could feel it, and it had been a while. "I need to get back out to Jason."

"Sam is there. So are AJ and Balta," Jonesy said. "Chill. Breathe a minute, because shit is gonna hit the fan, Andy. But your crew is rallying."

He looked up to Beau, who gave him a nod. "They can't fight us all. They won't. They'll want to spin this to suit them. Trust me. I'm with you."

Beau and Balta—they were three-time champs. They were on his side.

"Are you fucking kidding me?" Bax heard Kynan's voice raised in the hall outside, then the slam of maybe a helmet against the wall. "I got beat by a fucking crippled blind dude?"

Bax saw red, and he was up and out before Beau could catch him, barreling into Kynan. "You don't call him that!"

"What part of it is a lie? Oh wait—fucking crippled blind queer dude!"

The sound of his fist hitting Kynan's jaw was fucking amazing—and it felt pretty good too. He was going to clean the floor with that fucker once and for all. "No one even likes you," Bax screamed.

"Jesus, Andy!" Jonesy grabbed his arm, and Kynan took a swing, that Beau caught, whipping the kid around and forcing his hand behind his back.

"Walk it off, kid. You take it outside and walk it off, and I won't beat you so bad you aren't recognizable." Beau's voice was ice cold.

Kynan scoffed, but when Beau let him go, he was surrounded. Beau and Raul, Cotton and Hank. "Fucking old school bastards."

"Go on. Go lick your wounds. You'll be old soon enough." Beau's lip curled. "If you're lucky."

"Sim. Until he finds out we all get hurt at some point, no?" Raul stuck out that barrel chest, and that was it. Kynan stomped off.

Bax rubbed a hand over his ribs, which were bleeding again. "Sorry," he muttered to all and sundry.

"Go get Bax a clean shirt, Cotton. I'll finish taping him up." Jonesy took him back to sports medicine. "Now, you need to keep your cool. When Jason leaves, he's gonna need to be able to tell the reporters when and where his press conference will be."

"I was gonna take him home."

"Not now. News is already out. He'll need to spin. Dillon is already out with Coke. So you need to talk to someone about getting a PR guy. Stat. Maybe talk to Steele."

"Okay…" He couldn't do this.

"I will do it. I will call Steele and Daniel, my publicist now." Balta sounded calm as a still pond. "Sam brings Jason. We will talk to the press tonight. Seven o'clock.

Then the rest is by phone. Daniel will help. Beau and Sam will help."

"I'll go get my truck," Hank said. "None of these folks care about me. Y'all can sneak off in it, and I'll drive yours back to the hotel."

Jason walked in with Nattie, Sam and Ace, his lips tight and eyes hidden behind the dark glasses.

"We need to talk, Jason," Ace started in.

"We will. I need a shower. We'll meet at—what, Bax? Five-thirty?"

"Yeah. Balta is arranging the press conference at seven, probably at the hotel, if they got a room. That gives us time." See him just brazen it out.

"I want to be in on that."

Jason stood there, his hand on Bax's arm. "We'll talk at five-thirty. I'm leaving now. I need a shower. I need to find out about Gramps."

"Hank is getting his truck for us." Bax turned his back on Ace, because he couldn't cope with that expression. He could hear Balta talking hard. Beau was babbling at Ace and they just slipped away.

Bax put on the shirt he'd been handed before they got to the outside door, and they slipped out into the crowd of people at the back. The reporters weren't there yet.

Jason didn't say a word. He just walked one foot in front of the other, jaw set.

Hank pulled up seconds later. "Gimme your keys. AJ and I will get your gear." He handed over the truck, trusting them.

It didn't take seconds before they were loaded up and moving, and they were on the road before Jason asked, "Gramps?"

"He's at the hospital. That's all they had so far. Scans and X-rays. Can you voice text Dill and see if it's okay to call?"

"Yes." Jason barked orders at his phone, and Dillon immediately called.

"He's awake. It's his fucking back. Cracked two vertebrae, right between his shoulder blades. He's got sensation, movement. They're taking him into surgery in a few. But he's awake. He's pissed, but he's awake."

"Thank God," Bax said. "We got a meeting with Ace and a press conference. What do you need after that? We can bring shit to the hospital."

"I already called the hotel and added some days for me. If I need you, I'll holler, but you two need to deal with the fallout. Call Emmy."

"Balta's calling his publicist."

"Perfect. Call Emmy. You want her there."

"I'll call her now." Jason swallowed hard enough that Bax heard it. "Dillon, I'm sorry. I swear to God, I didn't mean to—"

"No." Dillon's voice was firm. "He did his job. You did yours, Jason. You won. We'll come to the beach and you can make it up to us by feeding us our weight in shrimp and brisket. Got it?"

"Y-yeah. You know it. I'll feed you both. I swear to God." Jase was fixin' to lose it.

"Okay. Coke and I love you guys." Dillon's voice finally broke. "I have to call Nattie. Call Emmy. I'll see you soon."

"Yeah. After the press." Jason hung up the phone, then sat back. "I don't know what to do, Andy."

"I know. Jesus, Mini. Jesus." He was blown, his hands shaking on the wheel. "We gotta do what's next."

"Right. It was supposed to be amazing. A celebration."

He pressed a hand to Jason's leg, inching through the traffic. "It will be. We just lost a little control of how things happened."

"They started the money transfer. That part is live." Jase swallowed. "Are you hurt bad?"

"No. You?"

"My head hurts, I still can't see, but besides that? I'm okay."

"Cut on my ribs."

His phone buzzed, and he looked since they were moving slow. "Cotton says Emmy will be there for the meeting with Ace. He already talked to her. Guess we get to meet those babies."

"Guess we will. I know it isn't as…right, I guess, but I did it. We did it. Together. We're champions."

"We did, baby." They hit a red light, and he leaned over, tugging Jason to him to take a light kiss. "We did it. The rest is just spin. I love you."

Jason nodded, and a ghost of a grin touched his lips. "Ditto, babe. I couldn't have done it without you."

Bax just snorted. "I know."

Chapter Twenty-Five

There was no way he was going to survive this. Jason puked up his guts, showered then got himself ready to enter the lion's den. He had no doubt that Randy would be there with Ace, along with Steele and Cash and a handful of the other founders.

Not Coke, though. Coke was in the fucking hospital.

He wore his sponsor shirt—the good white one that made him look taller, and a pair of Luccheses that sounded strong when he walked.

Bax never spoke a word.

Jase wasn't sure what had happened out on the arena floor. He'd been confused and overwhelmed and…and it had been over. He'd planned for this minute for the last two years, and now it was here and he'd lost himself.

He was sure as shit found now, though.

A knock came to the door, and when Bax answered it, he heard Emmy's voice. "Hey, guys. I brought Daniel. We're going to formulate a plan. Talked to Dillon. Coke is still in surgery, but it looks real good."

He closed his eyes a minute. *Thank God for that.*

"Come on in," Bax said. "I ordered up a catering tray. Should be here soon. I'm Andy Baxter, sir. Nice to meet you."

"Daniel Goodnight. Pleasure to meet you boys. Sorry it's under these circumstances. Let's all have a sit."

That smooth Texas drawl put Jason at ease. This was someone he could work with.

"I've spoken to Balta and to Miss Emmy here. Now I need to speak to you. What are your priorities?"

"I want my money and my title. I'm willing to announce my retirement today, but I'm not giving up the chance to tell my story." Dillon had told him that, and the sponsorships from that would be his money.

"That's more than fair," Daniel said. "The league will want to spin this in their favor, and if it's the money and the title that's important, I think you might be well served doing that—working together with them."

Jason nodded. "If they will, I will. If they want to play hardball, I will do that too."

Emmy was murmuring quietly to Bax, but he couldn't make out what they were saying. Not too much later, he heard her pounding something—maybe with her shoe—then the toilet flushed.

Daniel chuckled but was all business. "Good deal. So, we take the line first and foremost, that you clawed your way back up with no more help than anyone who had a catastrophic injury would get."

"You know it. I rode those bulls. Me. No one else." And he'd be damned if anyone argued.

"That's it. They're gonna argue all kinds of crap. You just keep that line. No spurs in the bull rope. Your rope is like everyone else's."

Emmy chuckled. "Yeah, they already examined it. You keep everyone but Coke out of it. That's what Dillon said. He knew. Coke knew. Andy knew. That's it."

"They're not going to believe that."

"Doesn't matter. They can't prove it." Emmy squeezed his fingers. "Coke knew. Andy knew. Dillon has an ironclad contract. You rode. Stick to that."

"I will." Jason could do that. That was a simple-ass story, and as far as not keeping Coke out, everyone would believe he wasn't gonna let something pass by. And Dillon knew if Coke knew. But they could keep it at that.

"I'll be in the meeting with you, Jason," Daniel said. "Emmy needs to stay out of it, as much as she can. She has a job to protect, and Cotton is still riding."

"Of course. How are the babies?"

"Beautiful. They're beautiful, and tomorrow I want you to meet them both. Adam and Brandon."

"I will. What does Taggart think of that?"

"Adam is tickled. Brian is mad at me." She chuckled. "Cotton's daddy was an Adam."

"That's sweet, honey." He was going to throw up again, and he knew he couldn't—not until after the press conference.

"You need a Coke, Mini?"

Maybe a little sugar would do him good. He was feeling shocky.

"Sprite?"

"I'm on it." Daniel moved fast. The man's shoes clicked and the door shut.

"You trust him, Em?" Bax asked.

"Yeah, so does Balta, and Balta's a biggie-wow."

"I know." Jason tilted his head. "What were y'all doing?"

"When?"

"With the smashing and the flushing."

Bax snorted. "Earpieces."

Oh. "Was that cheating? It didn't keep me on the bull."

"It's not, but we're not giving anyone anything, Jason."

"Okay." He nodded, making his head ache, and nausea burned again.

There was a soft knock at the door, Daniel coming back with drinks, he reckoned.

"Here, Mini." Bax handed him an open Sprite, and he took a grateful sip. The bubbles burned all the way down, clearing away the acid.

"When this is over, Daniel can set up interviews, all the complicated shit. You can go home. Get a dog. Learn braille. Enjoy your house. This is a blip, man. A little blip. Remember that. It seems big now, but…a little hiccup. You won." Emmy's voice was like an amazing preacher's, ringing with power and faith. "You fucking won, man. Blind and hurt and everything, and you kicked their asses. Remember that. *You* did this."

He took one deep breath, then another. Right. This was his. His and Bax's, and they couldn't take it, even if they tried. He was a fighter.

"She's right," Bax said quietly. "I'm right here. We got this."

"We do." They did. "I can't wait to go home and celebrate."

Bax gave him a one-armed hug. "So, Mister Daniel, do we let you do most of the talking?"

"Yep. Let me get the lay of the land. We can see what way the wind is blowing, since the big dogs have also had time to talk. But we stand firm."

"Bring it on." Jason was ready now. Get it over with. Rip off the Band-Aid.

They headed out, Bax at his side. If he had his way, Bax would be right here from now on, and damn the consequences. The room felt big, the voices echoing more, the air colder. There was more than Ace too, which he expected, but he was hoping for not too many folks.

"Jason, come, sit. Andy. Daniel, *bom dia*." Balta sure filled up all the available goddamn space.

He was damn relieved to hear that booming voice and know he had the big Brazilian in his corner.

"Hello, gents." Daniel helped him find his chair, Bax settling on his other side. "Ace. Cash. Steele. Been awhile."

"Figures he'd get a freaking Goodnight to look after him," Steele muttered.

Jason bit back a grin. He hadn't even thought about that. Looked like Daniel was cowboy royalty. That would help.

"Only the best, y'all." Daniel chuckled softly. "So, make your offer."

Yeah. Always get them to make their offer first, if possible.

"Offer?" Ace drawled out the word, and Jason could feel those eyes on him. He knew it like he knew his own hand.

"Yes, Ace. You want things. Spell it out."

Ace snorted. "Well, we want you to retire from riding."

"Jason is ready to announce," Daniel countered. "Tonight."

He nodded. He was. He was done with that part, and he wanted to go love on Bax forever.

"Okay, good. You can come with your sponsors, do signings for us even, but no more time behind the chutes, even to help other riders."

"The liability is a huge thing, son," Cash said.

"No problem." Cotton and Raul had Balta and Joa. "I'm good with doing signings."

"This could be disastrous for us as a league," Ace finally said. "We won't dispute your title or the payout, but we want a gag order. No books or movies or TV interviews or shows."

He started to holler, but Bax patted his thigh.

"No deal," Daniel said. "This is Jason's story to tell. You can decide how you want to play it, but the story is coming out. You want to be the good guys? You can say you knew. You can say you had zero idea. But no gag order. Period."

There was a long silence. Then Ace sighed. "We didn't know, and we can't act like we did. That would show preferential treatment. The main thing we have to show is that everyone had the same chance at the title."

"Well," Bax drawled. "They all had the same chances as Jason. 'Cept they could see."

Balta laughed, a booming sound. "Raul says he is fine with it. So who is to complain? Kynan? It was not his year. This we know because he fell off more than Jason."

"I rode those bulls. Y'all saw me. I rode. I wasn't superglued on. I rode those bulls." He didn't yell, because he didn't have to. He was right.

He heard Steele sigh too. "I told you, bud. You have to decide whose side you're on. Are you a cowboy or are you a suit?"

"Fuck you, Steele."

Daniel chuckled. "Well, he's got a point. You're here instead of the CEO because they're expecting you to protect their interests, Ace. I, on the other hand, have known you since your first junior bull riding. I expect you to protect the league only insofar as you want it to be a safe place for riders to do what they love."

"I hate all y'all," Ace grumbled. "And I don't believe for one minute that Andy here, and Pharris and the clown, are the only ones who knew. We'll say we had no idea and so will you. We'll make our own deal with Pharris. And we'll let the gag order go. Unofficially, however, I would like a consult on any projects you do, Jason. Not approval. Just a heads up about who, what and when."

"That's fair. I don't want to hurt bull riding. It's how I made my living. I love this sport. I paid dearly for it." And he wasn't paying any more.

"We can work with that, gentlemen. We'll draw something up, though, so the scope of your future involvement is clear." Daniel was a pro.

"What are you going to say to the press, Jason?" Cash asked.

"That I'm tickled I won, and I'm announcing my retirement." That was all he needed to say, right?

"I'll be giving the press the opportunities to ask me questions tonight, and I'll set up interviews starting next week, after he has a chance to get home." Daniel was slick as shit. Impressive.

"I'll be at the conference tonight," Ace said. "Just to have plausible deniability from the get-go."

"Sounds good. I'm glad we were able to come to a reasonable conclusion."

"I'm not a fucker, Dan. You know that," Ace said. "I just don't want to get fucked here, and I feel a little raw."

"Would you have let me ride, if you'd known?" Jason asked.

"Of course not."

"Then you understand why I didn't say."

"Hell, we all understand, Jason." That was Cash. "Ace woulda done the same thing. But we gotta make all these noises or we lose our jobs."

Steele cackled like a big old bird. "I personally love that you kicked everyone's asses, kid. I love it. You start a blind bull riding league, and I'll sponsor it."

"You are an asshole." Ace bit out every word, and Jason grinned. No one could tell they were best friends.

"I'll have something tentative drawn up by morning, y'all," Daniel said. "For right now, I need to get ready to meet the press."

"I'll see you here," Ace said. "Congratulations, Jason. Really."

"Thanks. Weirdest fucking finals yet."

Bax began to chuckle, the sound as familiar as his own breath.

Ace snorted. "I thought last year was pretty weird."

"Last two years," Cash muttered.

"No such thing as normal in bull riding, boys," Steele said. "I need to get to the hospital to see if Pharris needs anything."

"Can you take Dillon a burger or something? He'll be starving." He knew how hard Dillon had worked. He'd heard it.

"Absolutely. I'll call Nate on the way and see what they need." Steele clapped him on the shoulder, making him jump, then those boots clomped off.

Cash grunted. "I need to get back. Bulls to move. Holler if you need me, Ace."

"Rats deserting the sinking ship," Ace said.

"Nothing's sinking. We'll make a splash, that's all. There will be the flurry, then I get to have a real life. Hiding this was a bitch. I need to learn how to be functional, get the help I deserve."

Ace was silent a long moment, then he just said, "If you need help, you know where to find us."

"We do." Bax was right there. Solid as a rock.

"We do." He held out his hand. "Thanks, Ace."

Ace shook hands, then Daniel was hustling them back out of the room, on the phone before they were halfway back.

"You did good, Mini," Bax whispered.

"I need to hear about Gramps. I got him hurt."

"No. It could have been Kynan. Or Raul. That bull got him hurt." Bax said it fiercely, and it was partly true, but he'd frozen up and he knew it.

"I'll call Dillon again. He'll want to know what Ace said before Steele gets there."

Daniel left them at their room. "See you in an hour, boys."

He went in and sat, listening to Bax chatter to Dillon, but not hearing a single word.

He was done. He'd won…against the bulls and against his body.

Why didn't it feel better?

Why didn't he feel proud?

"Coke is out of surgery. He's resting."

"He going to be okay?" He needed to hear that.

"Dillon says he'll recover just fine." Bax sat next to him, then took his hand.

"I'm sorry."

"Coke says to smack you if you say that. They want us to come by on the way out of town."

"So you talked to him?"

"Yeah. He's just getting older, Mini. He's fixin' to go the way of us, I bet."

"I bet Ace asks him to." He sighed. "You heard what Cash said about liability."

"I did. And our liability is over. We do this thing, then it's over, Jason."

"It is. Can we leave in the morning after we see Coke?"

"Mini, you cain't see him, you're blind."

The words hit him just right and he started chuckling, then that laughter turned wild and happy.

Bax leaned into him and laughed with him, each one sending the other into new spasms when they stopped.

Finally they were clinging together, and Jason took a hard, happy kiss. "I love you, Bax. We did it. We won. Now we get to walk away."

"We do, babe. We do. I love you." Bax just hung on and knew exactly what his man was feeling.

Relief.

They'd survived.

Better than that, they'd won.

Chapter Twenty-Six

Bax stared down at the baby he held in his arms, fascinated by the faces the kid made as he slept. His lips moved, his forehead creasing—and he was working hard in there somewhere. Growing.

Jason held Em and Cotton's other baby, looking surprisingly relaxed. They were packed up, and from here they were heading to the hospital then home. They'd had a good talk with Emmy, and Balta and Raul had stopped by. Bax felt like he could start to relax.

"You look like you can breathe," Cotton said. "Congratulations."

"Thanks." He held the baby out to Cotton, who hooted. "Seriously. It's good. All but Coke."

"Emmy and me, we saw them last night. They stabilized his spine. He'll be going to pick up the dogs then come to you in a couple of days."

"Well, good." They would set it up so Coke didn't have to do dick all once he got up the stairs. "We've got tons of room for them and the bassets."

"I know Dillon appreciates it too," Emmy said softly. "Coke will need some enforced rest."

"They can stay right there with us, as long as they want to." Jason didn't sound the least bit hesitant.

Bax did love him so.

"I can't wait to see y'all's place come spring." Cotton wanted to come down and go deep-sea fishing.

"You're welcome, anytime. We do have stairs."

"We'll bring a baby gate if we need one, but I bet they're still pretty little in the spring, man." Cotton chuckled.

"They'll have a ball," Jason said. "Y'all just call."

"We will. We'll let you settle some after the holidays." Em gave them a husky chuckle. "Our families will want to see the babies a lot."

"Of course. Between your brothers and Cotton's momma, you're going to be on fire." Bax chuckled softly. "Come on, Jase. Let's go see Gramps and head home."

"You got it." Mini was subdued some, but he knew that was all about Gramps. Hopefully, seeing him would make it better.

Then he was taking his man home, dammit.

They'd earned this.

Bax was starting to feel like there was a damn conspiracy to keep them from starting the new part of their life. There wasn't, but he felt like it. He got Jason to give Em her baby back, then they were on the road.

"You get enough to eat?" Bax asked.

"Yeah."

Uh-huh. Right. Jason hadn't eaten a bite.

"You bring that muffin with you?" He needed Jason to at least try or he'd get sick on his stomach.

"Yeah. Yeah, I did. I love the lemon ones."

Jason needed to talk to Coke and go home. Go back to life—real, long-term life.

They had so much to do. Hell, Bax's honey-do list was longer than his arm. He was itchin' to get to work.

The hospital was an easy drive, and they parked in visitor's. "Come on, Mini. Let's go do this. The water is calling me." They wouldn't make it home tonight, but the day after that? They'd be in their own bed.

"I'm in." Jason stretched a little, and sure enough, halfway to the hospital Jason was eating that lemon muffin.

Coke was on the third floor, so they went straight up.

Dillon was sitting in Coke's room, and he glanced up when they came in, his drawn face brightening. "Hey, guys. Congratulations, Jason. You did it."

"I'm sorry. I swear to God, Dillon. I'm sorry."

Dillon shook his head. "It could have been anyone, Jason. Coke knows the drill. Let me wake him up so he can say hi, huh? They have him a little dopey so he doesn't move around too much."

"How bad is it?"

"He's tired, his body is wearing out, but he's going to heal. He can walk. He can feel his arms and legs. He just needs a break and a rest." Dillon stood and gently woke Coke up. "We're getting out of here in two days, then we fly home, get the dogs and head to you."

"That's right." Coke blinked awake. "We're going to have a nice long vacation, a rest."

Bax nodded easily. "You got it, Gramps. We got all the stuff you could need, huh?" He glanced at Dillon. "You gonna need any help driving down?"

"Nah. I'll be good. The pups are in Waco, but Nattie said he'll meet us with them and our truck in Houston. That's an easy drive to you."

"We'll come hang with you, see the doctors in Houston, spend some time." Coke met Jason's eyes, like that mattered. "They're going to make me retire, son. Ace came last night. I'm leaving. Nate is going to take over for at least a year. Dillon's got two years left on his contract."

Jason gawped toward Coke. "What? Gramps, you can't! Is this my—"

"Son, Jase— It's time. I'm ready. Me and Dillon and Nattie got plans to start a bullfighting school in Waco. We want to travel. We want to live. You understand that, don't you?"

"I do." Jason nodded, but his lips shook a little.

"We've been talking about it ever since Coke broke his neck last time. I'll take on an apprentice. I even have a few guys in mind," Dillon said. "Ace is willing to let me go early if the fans are positive about my replacement."

Lord. Shit always changed, but this seemed crazy. Crazy.

"Gramps, I—" Jason took Coke's hand. "I don't know how to do this."

"Yes, you do." Coke smiled at Jason, even though they all knew Jase couldn't see him. "You go home with Andy. You get a dog. You have a life. You know how to do this."

Jason stared at Coke's hand like he was really looking. "You think I can? I can—like, learn to use a cane. And a dog. I need you to tell me I can."

"I got no doubt. None at all. You won the championship without being able to see." Coke chuckled softly. "The rest is gravy." There was a second where Coke stopped, his lips twisted and he said, "I'm proud of you, Jason. You're the closest thing to a son I've ever had, and you did good. Now, go home and get ready for me to come for Turkey Day."

"I love you, old man."

"Good deal, because we're going to see a ton of each other."

Dillon watched them, a tiny smile on his face, and Bax felt all damn choked up. "Like a soap opera, y'all. Jesus."

"That's us, Andy. As the Cowboys Turn."

Jason chuckled. "The Young and the Bull Riders."

"The Bullfighting Light," Dillon added.

"Oh, for fuck's sake. All y'all have spent too much time over the years stuck in hotel rooms!" Bax groaned dramatically, and that got them all to laughing.

"Thank you. You and Dillon. For all your help." Jason squeezed Coke's hand, then squared his shoulders. "Y'all need anything?"

"I don't think so. Y'all will be home day after tomorrow. We'll be there a couple-three days after that. Pick me up some chocolate milk to take my pills with."

"We can do that." They would get all of Coke's favorites. Some of Dillon's too.

Dillon stood up with them. "I'll walk them out, babe."

"Good deal. Tell the nurse I want to get up and pee and have her change the sheets. I sweated."

"You got it." Dillon gave him double guns, then headed out with them, stopping by the nurses' station to murmur a few words. Then he joined them again. "This is not your fault, Jason. This is cowboy protection. We can't wait to come see you, though."

"You tell Nate if he wants to come for a few days too, he's welcome," Bax said. "I know he'll want to be home for Turkey Day, but we got time and room."

"Tracey wants to come out between the holidays, but they have some things to discuss." Dillon sighed softly, leading them to the elevators. "Coke was considering retiring already, Jase. He wants to start this bullfighting school with Nattie. Nate's going to sell his house and move out near us. This isn't your fault. Ace just made it so Coke didn't have to say it out loud."

"I'm gonna believe you, Dillon, because you wouldn't blow smoke up my ass." To Bax's ever-loving surprise, Jason reached out and snagged Dillon in a hug. Too bad Jason couldn't see Dillon's face. The man had clearly needed it.

"I'm ready for a holiday together. We're damn near family, right?"

"Shit, we are family—huge and fucked up and weird, but family." Jason snorted, tossing his head like a fractious horse. "We'll see you at the house in a few days."

"Go on." Dillon jerked his head at Bax. "Get him out of here before I get any more emotional."

"Yessir." Bax shook Dillon's hand. "You're a good friend, even if you freak me out a little."

Dillon did a little jig. "I love you too, Andy Baxter. Be careful going home."

They all chuckled then they turned and left. Coke and Dillon didn't need their dithering. Not one bit.

Jason reached out and took his arm, easy as pie, right there in the hospital. "I'm ready, Bax. Let's go home and get me a dog. It's time."

Bax snorted, then kinda busted out laughing. "Well, all right, Jason, but do they let all them hound dogs you love be seeing-eye dogs?"

God help them all… If it could be, Mini would make it so.

Bax led them out the door into the sunshine.

Their beach was waiting.

Want to see more from this author? Here's a taster for you to enjoy!

Rocking W: The Wounded Warrior

BA Tortuga

Excerpt

Matt took a deep breath, trying hard not to scream at his twin brother Luke. Shouting did more harm than good most days, but that fact didn't ease the temptation, really. The truth was that Matt needed help on the ranch, and Luke should've been able to do some of the lighter jobs, but he was still lying around on his ass feeling sorry for himself.

Guilt immediately clawed at Matt's gut. Luke deserved some downtime. Thirty-two missions with an eighty-two percent success rate meant nothing to Uncle Sam once that rate went down the toilet, thanks to an IED, a bunch of shattered bones, two surgeries and a scad of scars. Luke had given up a lot to be a SEAL and was now giving up even more of his life trying to recover.

So, instead of ramping up and stomping his damned boot heels, Matt counted to ten. "Hey, bud. I need some help with the foals."

"Help doing what? I'm no cowboy."

He peered into a face that ought to have been as familiar as his own, but somehow it wasn't. He was the older by eight minutes, but Luke seemed like he was in his forties, lines around his mouth that Matt didn't share, a hardness in his eyes.

"No, but you're what I got, and I need help." Luke was all about helping people, right? Matt was trying to appeal to his basic nature.

"Okay." Luke moved himself from the sofa to his wheelchair using his upper body strength, the heavy braces on his legs brutal as all get out. The doctors said he'd walk again without them and the crutches as long as Luke did his therapy, but Matt knew Luke didn't believe it.

Matt needed Luke to start believing.

Hell, he didn't give a living shit what the ornery son of a bitch believed in—Santa Claus, flying monkeys, yetis. He was easy. Matt wanted his easygoing, laughing twin back. Damn it, he was the quiet, serious one. The frickin' cowboy.

He held the door open for Luke, waiting for the wheelchair maneuver that caused the most trouble. Door jambs.

He'd fixed the ramp up, but the door would have to wait until he figured out where Luke was going to light for good. God knew his brother had always said he hated living in the back of beyond, which was why he'd gone into the Navy.

Luke managed to get out of the doorway without scraping his knuckles too bad. He'd suggested those fingerless leather glove deals, but Luke had responded poorly. His belly showed the bruises from Luke's no.

Luke still packed a hell of a punch.

They got down to the barn without too much trouble because Matt had graded the path a bit, and the foaling stalls would be a simple in and out, even with the wheelchair. He'd stabled a couple three foals when he fed, just to give Luke something to do.

The horses knew they were coming, hooves slamming against the dirt. In the barn, the whinnies started right away.

"They love you," he told Luke. "I don't fucking understand it."

Luke snorted. "They love the idea of some company, is all. Takes me longer to groom them, so I stay with them. They like that."

"Uh-huh." Matt didn't give a shit on the whys. He just cared about the love. His best mare, Shana, nosed over the stall door, her time in quarantine obviously chafing her. She had a cut just below her hock. "Hey, baby girl. How you doing today?"

He rubbed her velvet-soft nose, let her nibble on his palm.

She blew, bobbing her head up and down.

"Soon. I promise. Maybe today." He looked over at Luke. "You need help or you good?"

"I got it." Luke started with the last stall, and Matt headed out to check the yearlings.

He was beginning to think this whole thing was going to work, he really was. The horses were thriving—the cattle were working the back forty. All he had to do was hold on for a little longer.

* * * *

Luke would never tell Matt, but working with the horses soothed him deep down. Calmed his rage, for sure.

He had a lot of rage these days.

There was no way to be pissed around these long-legged beauties, though. No way in hell. The foal he was working with, a bay with a white star on her forehead, nuzzled his cheek, that nose so soft.

"Hey, sweet baby." He grabbed the brush and started working, making sure to touch the foal all over, gentling her as easily as he could.

She nibbled at him, curious but not nervous. She trusted him, and Luke felt honored. This was the one good thing in a mess of shit. He worked up a sweat grooming her to make up for the big plastic syringe of meds he was going to stuff down her throat.

It was necessary, though, and Matt was a psycho about taking care of things—horses and broken soldiers and Dad and everything.

He did love Matt for it—he really did. Luke grinned. Loved Matt, but wanted to beat him.

Like, with a hammer.

He chuckled when the foal lipped at his shirt because he'd stopped.

"You greedy girl, pushing me."

She snorted hard, blowing his pocket open. Yeah, she was hunting treats.

"So smart!" He rubbed her ears, giving praise. He could hear Matt in the pasture, whistling up a storm, the sound as familiar as his very bones, sunk deep into Luke's skin. His chest tightened, because he loved his brother, damn it, and that was what kept him going right now.

The whistles stopped for a half-second and he knew Matt was wondering if he was okay, if Matt should come check on him. Luke held his breath, willing Matt to just go back to work. Fine. He was fine.

Sometimes being a twin sucked. When he'd learned all he wanted to know about shrapnel, Matt had been in the ER with a migraine bad enough that he'd been convulsing. There was a thing between them, whether or not they wanted it.

The whistling started up again, and if it sounded strained, well, who was gonna mention it?

Not him, sure as shit. He just wanted to play with the foals and pretend he wasn't broke-dick.

The foal's head lifted, the sound of a pick-up truck that wasn't Matt's humming in his ears.

"Oh, goddamn motherfucker." Matt's words floated in, carried by pure rage.

Interesting.

He eased out of the stall after giving a piece of apple to the foal, and rolled to the barn door to peek out. A shiny black GMC king cab sat out there, and a man stood next to it, his pressed Wranglers and suit coat speaking money.

Now, who the hell was this and why did Matt look like he was fixin' to open a can of class A certified whup ass?

The guy was young enough, maybe early thirties. He had pretty smile lines and a flat belly under big silver buckle, and he was giving Matt a wry grin. "Now, don't be sore, Matt," he began. "You're still having trouble making payments and you know it."

"Go to hell, McConnell. Shit, go to fucking Arkansas. I don't care, but get off my land."

"They're going to drive you off, Matt. It's inevitable. I'm trying to get you a fair deal in the process."

"No, you want that acreage and that's all you give a shit about." Matt slapped his hand against the hood of the pick-up. "Off."

"You are one stubborn, stupid asshole, Matt Blanchard."

Oh, now. That was getting personal. Luke wheeled out into the yard, following the path he knew Matt had graded for him. "Who the hell are you to call my brother an asshole?"

"Must be the soldier come home from the war. Thank you for your service."

"I was a sailor."

"Right." The guy chuckled. "Rory McConnell. I went to school with your brother John."

He tilted his head. John was the baby, a good five years younger than them, eight years younger than Mark. "You're just a baby, then."

"It's not the age, it's the experience." Rory winked at him, blue eyes merry. The expression made Luke want to smile back, except that this guy had called Matt an asshole.

"Get off my land, McConnell. I mean it." Matt sounded about as mean as a snake. Luke glanced at him, noticing the narrowed eyes and pressed-together lips.

"I'm going. I'm not trying to be a dick, Matt. I'm really not. Better to sell now than to get your ass foreclosed on, you know? Just think about selling me that back fifty acres, if nothing else." McConnell slapped the hood of his truck before walking back to the driver's side door.

"Sell? Foreclosed? What the fuck, Matt?"

"I missed a few payments back when Dad went in the hospital." Matt's shoulders drew up around his ears. "I didn't want to worry you."

The big pickup pulled out in a rush of gravel and exhaust, McConnell not smiling now.

"Matty! I got cash. I wouldn't fucking leave you hurting."

"I know that, Lu. I do." Matt relaxed enough to give him a wry smile. "You also have a long recovery ahead of you and the VA sucks."

"Yeah, yeah. How much? And don't lie."

Matt swallowed hard, his throat working visibly. "I'm catching up. I am. I was three months in the hole and I still owed half the taxes. I only owe about three thousand."

"I'll give it to you. I can write you a check right now."

Matt's mouth took on a stubborn, flat line. "I can do it. I've got a sale coming up, and I think that one yearling I have will pay off the whole back debt."

"Fine, but let me cover it until you do. Hell, I'm staying here, eating your food, everything. Let me have some fucking worth, would you?"

Matt blinked for a moment, then nodded, coming to put a hand on his shoulder. "Okay, Lu. I get it. I do. We'll draw up a quick loan, though. So, you're actually the owner if I default somehow."

"What? We're going to be partners now?" He smiled, though, because the thought didn't suck.

A slow smile spread over Matt's face. "Would that work for you? I like the idea."

"Don't you grin at me, Matty." Still, they just grinned at each other like monkeys.

"Yeah. Well. Let me finish with the yearlings and we'll clean up and go into town. We'll need a notary."

"Does that mean you'll feed me Mexican?"

"Hell, yeah. I'll even spring for El Chico." Matt gripped his shoulder a moment longer, the gratitude clear in his expression. "Did you finish up with the babies?"

"I got one to dose, that's it. I was wondering what the fuck was up with McConnell there."

Matt snorted. "He's in some development war with that asshole Doug Harris down at the bank."

"Development war? Here? Are you shitting me?"

"Nope." Matt sighed. "Harris bought up about three hundred acres before anyone knew what he was doing. This place is like the iceberg blocking his cruise ship or something. McConnell owns about fifty acres behind us, but there's no road access. It was a stupid buy. I reckon he's going to try and buy me—us—out and then sell to Harris and make a fortune."

"Well, he can't have it. Either one of them." Luke put on his determined face, knowing it would make Matt laugh.

"No. No, this is ours." Matt grinned when he said 'ours'. Hugely. "Okay, get the dosing done. El Chico awaits."

"Dude, tableside guacamole and apple pie."

"You pig."

"Oink oink." Luke winked before turning his chair and rolling back to the barn. He felt better than he had in weeks, as if he finally had a purpose.

He wasn't sure what the fucking purpose was, but at least he had one. For right now, he'd take it.

PRIDE
PUBLISHING

About the Author

Texan to the bone and an unrepentant Daddy's Girl, BA Tortuga spends her days with her basset hounds and her beloved wife, texting her buddies, and eating Mexican food. When she's not doing that, she's writing. She spends her days off watching rodeo, knitting and surfing Pinterest in the name of research. BA's personal saviors include her wife, Julia Talbot, her best friends, and coffee. Lots of coffee. Really good coffee.

Having written everything from fist-fighting rednecks to hard-core cowboys to werewolves, BA does her damnedest to tell the stories of her heart, which was raised in Northeast Texas, but has heard the call of the high desert and lives in the Sandias. With books ranging from hard-hitting romance, to fiery menages, to the most traditional of love stories, BA refuses to be pigeon-holed by anyone but the voices in her head.

BA Tortuga loves to hear from readers. You can find her contact information, website details and author profile page at https://www.pride-publishing.com

Made in the USA
Coppell, TX
30 May 2021

56525293R00141